BOOTLEGGERS
& Basil

E.B. Wheeler

Rowan Ridge
Press

BOOTLEGGERS
& Basil

Other books by E.B. Wheeler

The Haunting of Springett Hall
Born to Treason
No Peace with the Dawn (with Jeffery Bateman)
Yours, Dorothy
Letters from the Homefront
The Bone Map
Utah Women: Pioneers, Poets & Politicians

Bootleggers & Basil © 2019 E.B. Wheeler

First printed as "The Picture Bride" in *Pathways to the Heart,*
published by Cedar Fort Media © 2017

ISBN 978-1-7321631-3-3

First printing: October 2019
Published by Rowan Ridge Press, Utah
Cover and interior design © Rowan Ridge Press
Front cover photos: dancer © dimitrisvetsikas1969, Salt Lake
City Main Street c1900 from Apollomelos-commonswiki
(public domain)

To Dan, for sharing my odyssey with me

Chapter One

HELEN CLUTCHED A PICTURE of her betrothed and wondered what her future husband would be like. Yiannis. His name was Yiannis. She looked again at the dark eyes staring at her through the portrait, trying to decipher what she saw there. His sternness reached through the photograph to stir nervous flutters in her chest. Maybe he'd been tense posing for the photographer. She'd been terrified when having her own picture taken to send to the stranger she was going to marry.

"Approaching the Rio Grande Depot, Salt Lake City!" the train porter called.

Helen fumbled for the handles of her bag, though it would be a few minutes before they arrived. She leaned toward the window, hungrily taking in the glimpses flashing by of snug little homes with gardens and a haze-wreathed city dominated by a great castle-like building.

She'd watched the land of opportunity glide past on her journey: the dizzying skyscrapers of New York, the suffocating green forests of the east, and the lonely and vulnerable flatness of the Great Plains. Here in the West, the arid landscape and springtime flowers reminded her a little of Greece, but everything was too new. Even the mountains here were young—still sharp and tall, not worn and stooped with age like the hills of Greece. In this familiar-but-foreign landscape, she had to hope there was a place for her.

She smiled to herself. No matter how strange it was, at least she would no longer be sitting on a hard bench that bit into her legs and left her backside numb. She hadn't had a chance to really stretch out since they'd left Denver.

An American woman sat across the aisle from her. She was dressed stylishly in a low-waisted dress with her blonde hair bobbed. Still, she didn't look much like the outrageous flappers Helen had been warned about.

Helen smoothed her own long, loose-fitting dress—rumpled after weeks spent in her bag—and adjusted her headscarf. The dress was the finest thing she owned, embroidered herself during the few moments around sunset when she'd had the luxury to dream of the future. A future where she was more than an unneeded younger daughter.

"That scarf will never do," a deep voice said in Greek.

Helen gave a start and looked at the dark-haired man sitting on the bench behind her, watching her with a quirky smile in his amber-colored eyes.

"Excuse me?" she asked. He hadn't said a word to her on the day-and-a-half long trip, though she'd noticed him in the pre-dawn gloom when she boarded in Denver.

"The headscarf. It's too old-fashioned. You need to get a hat like the American ladies." He gestured with his eyes to the other women sitting on the train.

She studied his face—handsome, she had to admit, and not much older than herself. "Do I know you?"

"I doubt it. Demetrios Nikolaides, at your service." He grinned and rested his elbows on the back of her seat.

Perhaps living in America had made him mad.

"I'll thank you to leave me in peace, Mr. Nikolaides. I'm on my way to meet my husband."

"I guessed as much. A picture bride." He leaned back and stretched his arm across the empty seat next to him. "I hope the picture he sent you was really his own. A lot of men send a false one to lure their pretty brides over, and once they get here, there's nothing to do but go forward." His grin widened. "I imagine you sent your real picture. You have nothing to be ashamed of, anyway."

Helen stared at him in horror. "Your Greek is good, but you have adopted some terrible American manners."

His gaze turned more serious. "I suppose you may be right. I do not know what I am—not Greek and not American. Soon you'll understand, too. It's too late to do much about it, but be warned that not everyone here is friendly to us Greek wanderers. We have to face our own cyclops and sirens, just like Odysseus."

She turned away, pushing aside the ominous warning, and secretly glanced again at the picture in her hand. Had Yiannis sent his own picture? Did it matter? As soon as she'd boarded the boat, her course had been set. She would marry Yiannis, even if he did not look like his picture. Besides, her cousin, Alexander, would not have let him send a false one.

Demetrios glanced over her shoulder. "Yes, that's probably the real thing. He would have chosen someone handsomer to fake the photo if that was his intention. Oh, wait!" He laughed. "That's Yiannis! I didn't recognize him all dressed up, with the soot and oil off his face."

"How do you know him?" Helen asked, trying not to think about a husband covered in soot and oil.

"The world is small when you are a Greek in Utah. And I really do think Yiannis would prefer you in a hat."

Helen glared and adjusted her headscarf as she turned away from the obnoxious man. The sooner she found Alexander, the sooner she would meet Yiannis. Then she could start her new life. Here, in the land of opportunity, she would finally find a place where she belonged.

The train lurched to a stop. Helen grabbed her

bag and pressed forward with the crowd exiting the train in Salt Lake City.

Cousin Alexander had warned her what to expect. An Italian band and singers would greet them. Helen thought that a very strange custom, but he assured her it was common in America, born of a friendship between Greeks and Italians forged in the mines and railroads. She would see her groom for the first time. They would be officially engaged, and the wedding would be on Sunday. Soon she would be a married woman with a home of her own. No longer a slave to her brother's wife and children. It would be hard work, yes, but it would be her own.

As she stepped onto the platform, she remembered Demetrios's teasing. She hoped Yiannis would be pleased with her appearance, though after weeks of traveling by steamship and train, she wasn't at her best. She also hoped she would be pleased with his appearance—and with his character. His face in the picture was not unpleasant, and Alexander had promised that Yiannis would make her an excellent husband. He was well off from working on the railroads. They would have a house with running water and electricity—luxuries Helen had never even dreamed of while hauling water from the village well.

The crowds pushed her along into the Rio Grande Depot, a soaring building with huge arched windows. She scanned each face, looking for one that resembled the cousin she remembered or the picture of Yiannis. Where were the greeting party and the Italian band? She shifted her bag from hand to hand and stood stupidly as the crowds dispersed.

What had happened? Perhaps they had been expecting her on the wrong day, though she had cabled ahead to tell them when she was supposed to arrive.

"Do you need help?" Demetrios stood watching her with sympathy.

"No," she snapped.

His gaze lingered, but she ignored him, staring straight ahead until he finally went on his way. She was tempted to jump right back on the train, but it would not take her back to Greece. She didn't have the money for the return trip. Certainly, everything would be fine. It was only embarrassing because that obnoxious Demetrios Nikolaides had witnessed it. Somewhere in this large city were her cousin and Yiannis. They would laugh over it later. She had endured Ellis Island, being poked and prodded and examined for lice and disease like a mule for sale; she could also endure this.

A figure emerged from the haze beyond the depot, and Helen stepped forward in relief. Alexander, come at last! But he was alone, his face stricken. He saw Helen, and his shoulders sagged. Had she disappointed him somehow? She clung to her bag. Had Yiannis seen her from afar and changed his mind?

Alexander threw his arms around her and held her so tightly, she dropped her luggage. "Oh, cousin Eleni. I am so sorry."

"Alexander?" she asked, her voice muffled by his coat. He smelled of smoke and oil like the city had seeped into him, and the fumes choked her.

He pulled away. "It's Yiannis." Helen held her breath, waiting for him to deliver the blow. "He's been killed."

"Killed!" Helen covered her mouth.

"In a railroad accident. Two days ago." His voice choked. "He was crushed. I'm so sorry."

Helen just stared, not knowing what to say. She couldn't focus. This railroad station, the smell of smoke, her dead bridegroom. They were all a dream, and she would soon awaken from it. "Killed?" she echoed.

"Come. The funeral is today. You should be there too. We will bury Yiannis. And then...then we must decide what to do with you."

His words penetrated the fog of unbelief. What to do with her? She was trapped in a foreign land with no money and no future. No one wanted her there, any more than they had wanted her in Greece. She lowered her head and followed Alexander without a word.

Chapter Two

ALEXANDER LED HELEN out of the train station to the confusion of the American streets. Men and women bustled by, automobiles and horse-drawn carriages competed for space on the road to pick up passengers, and the bells of streetcars rang out over the din. Helen stood for a moment, stunned by the chaos. Alexander gestured her toward one of the streetcars screeching to a stop on its tracks.

Helen hesitated. She had never ridden a streetcar before, but she imagined they were not free, and she had no money—just the handmade linens and a few pieces of family jewelry she brought into her marriage.

That had been the problem in Greece, too. No money for a dowry, so no one willing to marry her.

"Come!" Alexander called again, his voice as

impatient as the clanging of the bells.

She scurried over to him, nearly tripping on the rails laid over the street. Wires crisscrossed overhead as well, each tied to one of the streetcars like a leash. Her cousin paid for two tickets and handed one to her. She relaxed a little. If Alexander was wealthy enough to pay her way around, perhaps America really was a land of opportunity. She clutched her bag and stepped into the streetcar.

As soon as she was aboard, the car lurched forward. The few bench seats were full, so she clutched a pole to keep her balance, trying not to bounce against the men and women standing near her. Each time the streetcar swung around a turn, she had the opportunity to practice one of the English words she had learned before her journey: "Sorry."

She could hardly catch a glimpse of her new home, though she saw flashes of dirty streets and raggedly-dressed people not so different from Greek cities. The heads around her were blond and light brown, though, and the faces fair, pink, sometimes almost translucent—no familiar dark hair or olive skin touched by the caresses of the Mediterranean sun. Even Alexander looked paler than her, as if America had bleached some of the Greek out of him.

They zoomed past a department store with a sign reading ZCMI in huge letters and windows full of clothes. The streetcar reached the huge white stone building with six spires pricking the sky and turned past it to go uphill to a cathedral overlooking the city. Alexander helped her out, and the streetcar was off again.

Helen looked up at the cathedral and blinked in surprise. "This is a Catholic church."

"This is the best place we have to hold the funeral."

"Isn't there an Orthodox church here?"

"We sold the old one, and the new one isn't finished yet. We still have some meetings there, but this church has more space, and it's closer to Mount Olivet, where Yiannis will be buried."

He took off his hat and entered the church. Helen looked back over the hazy city below, then turned her gaze to the eastern mountains barring the way back to Greece. Mount Olivet meant the Mount of Olives, but there were no olive trees here—only soot and smoke in place of the familiar scent of meadows and sheep. At least the name sounded comforting. It would be a good place for her prospective groom to be buried. Again, an unreal sensation swept over her, and she expected to awake at any moment. But she did not, so she followed Alexander into the cathedral.

The somber reverence of the place stilled her taut nerves. Smooth pillars swept up to the ceiling far overhead, where they opened out like branches supporting the vaulted roof. Light poured through the colored windows showing familiar scenes from the Bible, and the air was rich with the scent of incense. It was strange stepping into a church belonging to the Catholics—like going to a quarrelsome cousin's house for an awkward dinner—but at least they weren't so different from the Orthodox Greeks.

A keening wail reminded Helen why she was there. Men wore their best suits and spoke in hushed voices where they gathered around the coffin. A priest, obvious by his dark robes and long beard, oversaw the somber gathering. A few women in traditional dresses and headscarves gathered around, singing the songs of mourning over Yiannis. Helen approached slowly. She had seen death before, but she felt suddenly shy, seeing the man she was supposed to have married only to bury him instead.

She peered into the coffin. As was the custom for single men, he was buried in what would have been his wedding clothes, and he wore a little pouch around his neck containing a pinch of Greek earth. His mother would have sent it with him for this very reason, hoping it would never be needed. There was little evidence he had died in an accident. His face looked solemn, as it had in his photograph, and also very sad. He had been pleasant looking. Helen wanted to apologize for not arriving sooner. Then he would have had someone to mourn him properly—family. Her eyes stung, and warm tears rolled down her cheeks.

Whispers rose behind her, and she quickly turned away from the watching crowd.

"You did make him happy," Alexander whispered to her. "He died looking forward to the wedding."

Helen nodded. She sat through the rest of the funeral with a stoic face, though she felt as though pieces of her heart and her hopes were snuffed out with each word. As the funeral came to a close, her chest tightened. When she stepped out of the cathedral, she was facing an uncertain future in a world where she didn't belong.

Chapter Three

"Come, Helen, it's time to go home," Alexander said as the crowd began to disperse from the funeral.

Helen gave a start. "Home?"

"Yes, to my home. My wife will appreciate the help."

"Oh." Helen followed him in a daze. So, she was to be a servant again, raising another woman's children, cleaning another family's house. She was grateful to have a roof over her head, but she ached for the loss of the home she had dreamed of on the long journey.

The babble of American English pressed around her on the streetcar. The little English she had learned when her family could spare her long enough to go to school in the neighboring village didn't sound much like the noise around her. She caught people staring at her and looked away, willing herself not to blush.

Finally, she and Alexander escaped the noise and stale stench of the streetcar, and her cousin led her down a block lined with small houses and coffee shops. The slightly-burnt scent of roasted coffee beans mingled with that of bread baking in outdoor ovens, and the aroma of basil growing in sunny windowsills welcomed her. Greek conversations drifted from the nearby houses, soothing Helen's frayed nerves.

Alexander led her into one of the little homes. Helen smiled to see an electric bulb dangling from the ceiling. It cast a bright, happy glow over the interior. Three young children ran about, giggling and calling to each other in a mix of English and Greek.

"Dear, I have brought my cousin home. Helen, this is my wife, Agatha."

Agatha gave her a quick, dismissive look. "Good. I can use some help in the kitchen."

Helen steeled herself with a deep breath. Yes, just like home.

"Fetch some water in that pot," Agatha said.

Helen picked up the pot and peered out the window. She hadn't noticed a well on her walk into the neighborhood.

Agatha rolled her eyes. "From the sink."

Helen followed Agatha's gaze and hurried over to the sink. How to make it work? She lifted the handle and fresh, clear water poured out. Helen had to remind herself not to gape and quickly filled the pot.

What a wonder! Having fresh water right in their home and not having to walk down to a village well every day to fetch it. America was a land of ongoing amazement.

That night, Helen slept on a mat in the children's room. As she listened to the children's quiet breathing, she thought over life in America. Here, she didn't have to haul water from a well. She was living in a house with electricity. The physical toll of her work would be lightened. In Greece, she had no future, because no man would accept a woman without a dowry, but here in America, there were so few Greek women, she might still capture someone's eye. It could be possible for her to find a new future, with a family and a home of her own.

Since Helen didn't have time to wash her travel-weary best dress before Sunday, she put on her second-best for church. The fabric was a plain blue, but she had sewn it herself, each stitch carefully placed. Alexander's family all wore crisply tailored suits and dresses.

Agatha stopped at the mirror to put on a hat with a little feather before stepping outside. A hat! Helen smoothed her headscarf. What did it matter what Agatha wore to church?

The entire Greek neighborhood converged on the unfinished Orthodox church building. Greek columns guarded the steps leading up to the entrance, and two round towers crowned the front corners. Someday, it would be beautiful, and its

Byzantine design was as familiar as the melting sweetness of baklava, but the tools and rubble of construction littering the grounds struck Helen as sacrilegious. Her church back home had been as ancient, it seemed, as the Greek words of the New Testament.

Inside the building, Helen clung to Agatha and the handful of other women, vastly outnumbered by the horde of men. The women gossiped, their hats almost touching as they whispered together, sometimes in English too fast for Helen to understand. Only one old woman wore a headscarf. She smiled a toothless grin at Helen, who wished she could pull her scarf over her eyes and vanish. In Greece, she had been considered pretty enough—her fatal fault was that she had no dowry—but here she felt as shabby and out of place as her plain, handmade dress. In Greece, her family's proud name of Botzaris—associated with those who fought for Greek independence—had meant something, but here she sensed it carried much less weight. She was playing a new game and did not understand the rules.

Despite her shabby appearance, some of the men watched her with interest. A little thrill rushed over her at being an object of attention, though she knew it was because she was one of the only single Greek women in the city. She would have to find a way to get to know more about the eligible young men, but there were probably no matchmakers here. How did one court in America?

The service, at least, was familiar, until Reverend

Karahales reached the end and invited John Condas to speak.

Helen gave Agatha a curious look.

"The president of the board of trustees," she whispered.

Helen wasn't sure what that meant and didn't dare ask. John Condas stood and reminded the congregation to continue contributing to the fund for finishing the church. He swept the congregation with an imploring glance. "And please, remember the great country that we represent." His gaze rested on a few individuals. "As long as you're here, be law-abiding citizens."

A wave of rustling and throat clearing rolled through the room, then John Condas sat, and the tension broke. Helen looked to her cousin for an explanation.

Alexander shrugged. "There has been a little trouble—nothing to worry yourself over."

"What kind of trouble?"

"Greeks and Americans do not always see eye to eye. Prohibition has been especially troublesome. Try telling a people from a land of vineyards that they cannot drink a little wine with dinner... Well, a few Greeks have been arrested lately for making their own alcohol—moonshine, the Americans call it. The police are watching us closely now." He hesitated. "There are others, too, who don't like immigrants coming to America. We hope, if we keep our heads down, they will leave us alone."

Helen frowned at the strangeness of America.

After the service, the congregation lingered.

Helen held back, trying to learn the patterns of her new life. A young woman dressed all in black approached her cautiously.

"You are Alexander Botzaris's cousin, are you not? The one who was supposed to marry Yiannis?"

There was no morbid interest in the woman's voice, only a gentle sympathy. Helen nodded.

"I'm sorry," the woman said. "I was a picture bride too." She met Helen's gaze, as though searching for understanding. "My husband died several months ago in the Castle Gate Mine explosion."

"I'm so sorry," Helen said. Greek widows did not remarry. Helen wondered how this woman survived.

"I'm Katherine," the woman said. She looked like she would have said more, but someone called her name. She smiled at Helen and hurried away. Helen was sorry to see her go.

Helen drifted back to Alexander's family and stood near Agatha, trying to hide under the comforting weight of her headscarf.

"Mrs. Botzaris," said a familiar voice behind her.

She turned with Agatha to see the Greek man from the train smiling at her. Her face flushed. Of course, Demetrios Nikolaides attended church with the rest of the Greek community.

"What a lovely hat you're wearing today." He spoke to Agatha with perfect seriousness, but laughter danced in his eyes, and Helen knew it was directed at her. She refused to meet his gaze.

"Thank you, Mr. Nikolaides." Agatha seemed a little befuddled at the compliment, which almost made Helen smile. Almost.

Demetrios nodded to both ladies and strode away. Agatha shrugged and said nothing about him, leaving Helen to try not to think about the way his amber eyes had lit up when he teased her. The last thing she needed was to have that troublesome man making her feel foolish at every turn. Well, when she had her own place—a settled role in the community—then he would have to leave her in peace.

Chapter Four

"TODAY, I'll send you out to wash the laundry," Agatha told Helen a few Mondays later.

Helen sighed inwardly. She'd spent the last three weeks trying to find tasks she could accomplish to Agatha's exacting standards. Alexander left early each morning and worked until late each night, so every day except Sunday, it was just Helen and Agatha and an unending line of chores, many of which were different from those in Greece. Helen's favorite part of the day was helping the children get ready for school, serving their breakfast and brushing their hair while they taught her more English.

Still, doing laundry for Greek bachelors was an important part of the family's income. If Agatha trusted her to do it, Helen must have finally gained her cousin-in-law's approval.

"The men leave their shirts by the back fence," Agatha said.

Helen thought that strange, but she started some water boiling on the stove and readied the washtubs outside near the beehive-shaped oven for the bread. It was a pleasant morning. Helen could almost imagine herself back in Greece, though the air here was sooty from the nearby smelters and factories. The sun sat lower in the sky than it had in Greece, and the light never seemed as brilliant.

When the water was ready, she fetched the clothes from the pile by the fence. As soon as she touched them, she understood why Agatha kept them outside. The sweat-stained shirts crawled with lice. Helen jerked her hands back and shook them off, though none of the little creatures had made their way to her skin. Was this what Greek men in America were reduced to? She had ridden the streetcar with all those Americans, and she didn't think they were so lousy.

She frowned and looked around the yard. A long stick lay near the fence. Holding it at arm's length, she used it to pick up the clothes and dip them into the boiling water. She rubbed her hands off, itching at the thought of the lice, and poured the lye into the steaming water. Agatha had left her a box of soap flakes. Soap was an expensive rarity in her village. The little brown flakes smelled luxurious. She sprinkled a few in, afraid to waste them. They seemed to make little difference in the stench of the steaming tub as she stirred the mess with her stick. Only when she was certain all the lice would be dead did she scrub the shirts on the washboard, rinse them in the second tub, and hang them to dry.

Agatha wrinkled her nose when she examined Helen's work flapping in the evening breeze. "Didn't you use any soap?"

"A little," Helen said sheepishly.

"Well, I suppose the smell will remind the men of home." Agatha shook her head.

Helen bit back a bitter retort. Laundry was not a source of pride for her, but she'd been doing it for years, and none of her family had ever complained. In America, even the simplest tasks made a fool of her.

The next day, Helen ironed all of the shirts. She heated the iron in the fireplace and took the time to make certain that no shirt had a single wrinkle or a crease out of place. By the time she was done, sweat dampened her face and her arms ached from the weight of the iron. She grimaced as she folded all those white shirts. By the end, she could do without ever seeing another one, but no one could complain that she did not know how to iron and fold shirts.

What an accomplishment, though. Laundress was not a job she aspired to. It wouldn't be so bad if she were just doing the laundry for her own husband and children, but for the whole neighborhood?

The next week, Helen was more liberal with the soap, and Agatha gave her a nod of approval when she surveyed the shirts flapping from the laundry line.

"When the men come to fetch their laundry and pay you, take the money to the store," she said. "We need more currants and a new shirt for Nikoleta."

Helen nodded, excited for the opportunity to get away from the house for a while. "Where is the store?"

"A block southwest of here."

Helen could find that easily enough.

As the men came throughout the day to collect the shirts, Helen gave each of them appraising looks. Most seemed glad to do business with her instead of Agatha, and she suspected they were sizing her up as the only eligible woman in the neighborhood. She tried not to think of the lice crawling through all of their clothes. The bachelors mainly slept in boarding houses, and they could not help being lousy. Having their own home would fix that problem.

They seemed to not know how to speak to a single woman, though. They probably had little practice since leaving Greece, and there they would have had the help of their family or a matchmaker.

One man handed her his coins, blushing bright red, and just pointed to the shirt that was his.

"Thank you," another man said. He fidgeted in the doorway. A fly buzzed past Helen into the house, and she grimaced.

"Um, you do nice washing," the man finally said and hurried away. Helen tried not to laugh at the poor fellow.

She wasn't sure how she was supposed to get to know any of them better. In America, most Greek women came as picture brides. Helen didn't fancy the idea of Alexander or Agatha arranging a husband for her, so she would have to discover how the Americans managed it. What did courting couples talk about?

She went to the store with a heavy purse. Some of the men had paid in canned fruit or coal, but enough of them had cash that she was excited to see what bargains she could find at the dry goods store. Luckily, the signs were in Greek: she would have no trouble communicating here. She stepped inside and was met by the homey aroma of basil and olives. She took a deep breath, letting the scents roll through her and fill her with the feeling of home. Then she opened her eyes and went to work.

The store was a tiny building, badly crowded with merchandise. She had to squeeze past a stack of Greek-language newspapers lying on top of a display of men's long underwear and then around a stand of umbrellas that snagged at her dress. It was like trying to escape from the Minotaur's maze. How did anyone find what they wanted? Eventually, she fought her way through to the center of the store, tripping once on a lumpy rug.

Where to start in this chaos? Buying the currants would be easy, so she headed instead for the shelves of women's clothing. She studied the prices and her coins to get a feel for the way American money worked. It amazed her to see so many ready-made clothes. She ran her fingers over the fabric in the display of women's dresses and wondered if she would ever have enough to buy one of her own. If she wasn't making any money and didn't have a husband to provide for her, she would have to keep wearing the same shabby clothes. She told herself it didn't matter—Greek men would still look at her, just because she was a Greek woman—but how lovely it would feel to wear something pretty and fresh.

Helen paused at the hats. They were attractive, forward, enticing. She glanced back at the bored-looking young clerk behind the counter, who was doodling on the Greek-language newspaper. She carefully untied her headscarf and placed the hat on, tilting it a little, then peeked in the mirror. The hat let her dark curls flow free and framed her face, bringing out her deep brown eyes.

"Charming," a deep voice said. Demetrios's face appeared in the mirror beside hers.

Helen scrambled for her headscarf and clutched it in front of her as she turned to face him. She'd managed to avoid him at church for the last few weeks; why did she have to run into him now? "What are you doing here?"

He smiled and leaned closer. He smelled like the brilliantine styling his dark brown hair, inviting her to step closer, inhale more deeply. She pulled back.

"I'm watching one of my customers try on a very fetching hat," he said.

"Your customer?" She glanced around. "This is *your* store?"

He grinned, and the laughter danced in his eyes. "It is. Didn't anyone tell you? If there's anything you need, Demetrios is the one to ask."

Helen whipped off the hat and tugged her scarf back on. "I just need a shirt for my cousin's daughter. And some currants." She raised her head.

"But the price for the shirt is too high."

"What will you do then? Go to an American shop?" He raised an eyebrow, a challenge glittering in his eyes. "You think you can get a better deal there?"

"I think I can make it myself if I must, but I won't pay such outrageous prices."

He chuckled. "Very good. Most Greeks forget how to bargain when they come to America. Or they get trapped by the company stores, and there's no bargaining there." He shook his head. "What will you give me, then, for the shirt and the currants?"

She named a price that was much too low, and he countered with a more reasonable one until they worked their way to the price she expected to pay. He went to the back to get the currants, and the young clerk made himself busy straightening the counter, his doodling forgotten.

Demetrios returned with the little sack of currants. "Here they are as we agreed. But only if you take the hat too."

"That hat?" Helen faltered. "I have no money for a hat. I don't need one."

"I'm not selling it to you. I'm giving it to you, and you only pay the price you named for the currants and the shirt."

"That makes no sense." Was he teasing her for her poverty? She had a respectable name, and she did not need his pity. "You are mad."

He chuckled. "Not at all. I am doing what pleases me. You looked quite fetching in that hat."

Helen narrowed her eyes. "I won't have anyone

playing games with me. I don't want the hat." She thrust her coins into his hands—more than they had agreed upon—and took the shirt and the currants, leaving the hat behind. She turned and wriggling her way past the displays and out of the shop. Demetrios's laughter rang in the store behind her. Insufferable lunatic!

Chapter Five

THE NEXT SUNDAY, Helen helped the children get ready for church before she dressed herself. She welcomed the familiar rituals of the Sabbath after a long week of hard work: more cooking, more scrubbing, more laundry. For all the conveniences of America, the work never stopped.

Helen rubbed a little olive oil into her skin to soften her hands and gently lifted her headscarf. The edges displayed a string of embroidered birds taking flight. She had tried to capture that glorious moment when their beating wings first lifted them to the freedom of the skies.

As she covered her hair, she thought of Demetrios's hat but quickly dismissed the thought. What silly vanity that was! She had too much pride to let him know that she wanted it. Or to accept any gifts from him—gifts that would just make him laugh at her. A memory of the way his eyes danced when he laughed flashed across her mind, but she shoved it aside. At church, she would have a chance to mingle with other men in the Greek neighborhood and visit with the widow Katherine again.

She stepped out of the children's bedroom to find Agatha standing in the parlor, clutching a box, her lips pressed in anger. Before Helen could ask what was wrong, Agatha whirled on her.

"What's the meaning of this?" Agatha shook the box.

Helen looked inside. "It's a hat," she said faintly. Not just any hat. The one she had admired at Demetrios's shop.

"A hat delivered to you by Demetrios Nikolaides. How did you pay for it?"

Helen blanched. Did Agatha think she'd been stealing from her? She'd brought back the change from her exchange with Demetrios. Despite turning down his offer, she'd made a good bargain and had been proud of herself. Agatha had seemed pleased too. "I didn't buy it. I guess he saw me admiring it and wanted me to have it."

"Wanted you to have it? Ha! Not Demetrios. He's all business. He doesn't do anything unless there's something in it for him." Her voice turned icy as she narrowed her eyes. "What did you do to earn this from him?"

Helen gaped, realizing what Agatha was implying. "Nothing! I did nothing!"

"Don't lie to me. Nothing stays a secret for long in Greek Town. If you did anything to disgrace the Botzaris family name..."

"It was my name before it was yours!" Helen shouted. The neighbors could probably hear. She didn't care. "Do not tell me how to care for it." She lowered her voice. "He gave me the hat to humiliate me. To remind me that I have nothing of my own. Does that please you?"

Agatha shoved the hat at her and stormed away. Helen stifled a sob and rushed into her room. She was tempted to throw the hat in the gutter, but then everyone would see it. She stowed it instead inside her bag and checked the little mirror to make sure her eyes showed no tears.

The family marched to church in stony silence, gaining curious looks from their neighbors. No doubt they would fuel the neighborhood gossip for the rest of the week, if not longer. If only Demetrios did not hear of it. Helen did not want to see him laugh at her again.

They sat through the church service, the words buzzing around Helen's ears without finding any place to land. Her whole concentration was on looking calm and ignoring the stares she felt directed at her and Agatha.

As soon as the service was over, she tried to make her way out of the church. Demetrios cornered her before she made it to the exit.

"Please let me go," she whispered.

"What has happened? Didn't you receive my gift?" He asked. There was a hint of amusement in his voice.

"Your gift!" Helen's voice echoed off the unfinished walls. She squeezed her eyes shut, and when she opened them, there was no laughter in his eyes. "Your joke has cost me enough already," she said quietly. "Please do not speak to me again."

She pushed past him without meeting his gaze and rushed outside. The hazy air made her squint. Beyond Greek Town, people strolled by in their Sunday best and the bells rang on the streetcars. Oh, how she longed for her village in Greece! There, the rules were clear, and she never would have been so humiliated.

A gentle hand touched her arm. She jumped and turned to find Katherine watching her with sympathetic eyes, her pale face offset by her black mourning clothes.

"Do you want to tell me about it?" Katherine asked.

Helen shook her head, but a glance at Katherine's understanding gaze and the whole story came spilling out.

Katherine put an arm around her, and Helen leaned into the comfort of a friendly shoulder, like having one of her sisters back again.

"Demetrios is a stubborn fool," Katherine said. "He thinks he knows what's best, and he's forgotten too much of Greece to understand why he's wrong."

"It doesn't matter why he did it," Helen said. "I have never been so embarrassed. How can I live with Agatha, knowing she thinks I'm the kind of woman who would disgrace myself and my family name?

And over a hat!"

Katherine smiled. "There will be some new gossip or scandal soon enough, and this will blow over, especially because everyone knows how Demetrios is. As for Agatha..." Katherine gave Helen a heavy look, as though she were wrestling with some weighty secret. "This may be hard to consider, but why not live somewhere else?"

Helen pulled back to stare at Katherine and laughed a little. "Where would I go? I have no other family here. Not even the means to go home to Greece."

"Do you want to go back?"

"Yes." She hesitated, imagining the shame of returning home a single woman. "I don't know."

"Listen. I know how important tradition is, but in America, things can be different. You could get a job, support yourself."

Helen stared at her. "A job? Doing what?" In her village, the only work for women was taking care of their families or minding the goats—the unclean animals the men did not want to tend.

"Do you speak much English?"

"I understand a lot now, but I...I feel shy speaking it, and the words get twisted up in my mouth," Helen admitted.

"Hmm. That rules out telephone operator, then. You're pretty enough to work in a department store, but not until you're more confident with English and save enough to buy some modern clothes. In the meantime, there are many factory jobs."

Helen flinched a little at the thought of the

smoke pouring from the factories, but she was intrigued. "Doing what?"

"Oh, all kinds of things. A lot of Italian girls work in the bakeries and the macaroni factory. I dip chocolates in one of the Greek candy shops."

Helen perked up a bit at that. She'd only tried chocolate once, but it had been heavenly.

Katherine hurried on. "There are no openings at my shop right now—the Americans have accused us of making impure candy, and we are struggling. But the other girls and I, we can look around for you. The canneries aren't bad, but they're not doing as well right now—the farms in Utah have struggled since the war ended." Her eyes brightened. "Do you weave or sew?"

"I do."

"Perfect. There are several textile and knitting factories. They're always looking for more girls to run the machines."

"Machines?" Helen asked. She had only sewn by hand.

"Don't worry—they'll teach you how."

"Yes, I'd like that." If Helen earned money, then she could buy her own dresses and hats—from the American shops, not Demetrios's. "But how do I tell Agatha I won't be working for her while I'm living under her roof?"

"You won't be. You can come to the ladies' boarding house with me."

Helen lowered her voice. "Is that respectable?"

"Very much so. A few other girls live there. An Italian widow runs it, and she's very strict. No improprieties allowed." Katherine looked concerned for a moment, but she shook it off and smiled. "Most of the girls are Italian, but there's one other Greek girl there. You'll like it. It's in Little Italy, just west of here, by the Rio Grande Depot, so not too far to walk to church. You just have to show Mrs. Alberti that you have a job, and she'll rent you a room. She's a great cook too."

"Thank you!" Helen embraced Katherine and looked back over Salt Lake City. It promised a whole new kind of hope now. Her heart beat faster— nervous excitement pumping through her body and lifting her spirits. "I'll start looking tomorrow."

Chapter Six

HELEN HELPED THE CHILDREN dress for school in the morning, then hurried to get herself ready. It helped that Agatha wasn't speaking to her except to issue an occasional command. Helen put on her blue dress and hesitated over her headscarf. She wanted to look modern, and a headscarf might not be safe around machines. Glancing over her shoulder, she pulled out Demetrios's hat and secured it over her long, wavy black hair. Guilt gnawed at her stomach.

"I'm just borrowing it until I can buy one for myself," she whispered to her reflection. "He'll never know."

She forced a smile at the mirror and almost didn't recognize her more modern-looking self.

The hallway was clear, so she fled out the front door, shutting it quietly behind her. Clutched in her hand, she held the addresses of the nearby textile mills. Helen marched down the street, aware that some of her neighbors would likely see her and Agatha would hear about it before the end of the day. She had to have a job by then or her life would become a constant stream of arguments with her cousin's wife.

She had no money for a streetcar, so she walked to the first factory. The racket in the building pounded her ears like the noise of propellers on a ship—a ceaseless, pulsing roar. Lines of girls kept their heads bent over sewing machines, pushing fast streams of fabric under flying needles. Helen hoped she could get the hang of the machines without punching the needle through her fingers. She pressed forward, looking for a man who seemed to be in charge.

"Pardon!" she shouted over the noise. "Pardon!"

The man looked over at her with a bored expression. "What do you need, miss?"

She had practiced these words carefully. "I need a job."

The man squinted at her. "You Italian?"

She couldn't hear well over the machines, but she caught "Italian," so she nodded.

His face darkened, and he shouted a string of words in her face she didn't understand and didn't want to. She hurried off before he had a chance to say more.

Apparently, being Italian wasn't a good thing. At the next factory, it was quieter, but the man in charge kept saying, "closed shop," which Helen didn't understand because the shop looked open, but it seemed to mean that there were no jobs for her there either.

She approached the last address, her stomach a tight knot. She said a prayer to Mary, the mother of the Lord, and approached the man overseeing the workers. He was speaking loudly with another man, so Helen hung back, observing the factory. Here, the girls were running looms. The back and forth of the giant machines soothed her, and the loud whooshing and clacking were not as intimidating as the other factories. This would be it. It had to be.

The foreman turned away from his conversation, shaking his head. Helen sensed it wasn't a good time to talk to him, but as she tried to back away, his gaze fell on her, and he narrowed his eyes.

"What are you doing lurking around here? What do you want?"

"Job," Helen croaked out. She tried again, more boldly. "I need a job."

"I bet that's all the English you know," the man said. "How do I know you can do the work?"

Helen hesitated, trying to put together the words she knew but was afraid to say incorrectly. "I weave," she said. "I weave. I need a job."

"Huh. I don't have time to train some idiot girl who can't even learn to speak English."

Helen didn't know all the words, but she understood his intent. She couldn't quit, though. She couldn't go back to Agatha's house without a job. She stepped forward. "I weave. I work hard. I learn more English."

The man rolled his eyes and turned away.

"Wait!" A familiar voice shouted behind Helen.

She gave a start as Demetrios strode past her to start arguing with the foreman. She cringed. He had been the one talking with the foreman when she had arrived. Now, he was a witness to her humiliation once again. And she was wearing his hat! She turned to slink away, but a firm hand on her shoulder stopped her. Demetrios spun her around to face the foreman.

"She's a respectable girl and a hard worker," he said in English. "If you don't want Greeks to make your fabrics, why should I buy cloth from you to sell to Greeks in my store? You can forget the deal we made. I'll take my business elsewhere." He turned away, dragging a baffled Helen with him.

"Wait!" the man called. He bustled over to catch up with Demetrios. "I ain't got a problem with Greeks. I just don't want to waste time training some girl who's too dumb to understand, or who's going to get married and disappear a few months later. American girls stick around longer, especially if they're already married."

Demetrios smiled. "I can't make any promises about her not getting married, but I guarantee she's brighter than most of the workers you already have."

The man shrugged. "If you say so, Demetrios. I just lost one of the girls who worked on the looms anyway."

Demetrios nodded and shook the man's hand. Helen didn't understand everything that had just happened, but the man motioned for her to follow him. Demetrios gave her shoulder one last squeeze, and let his hand linger there for a moment. His touch sent a warm shiver through her, and she flushed and pulled away. She looked up, prepared to thank him as gracefully as she could manage, but stopped at the sight of his grin.

"That hat really is quite charming," he said in Greek.

Then he was gone, and she was left to hurry after the impatient foreman. She had to banish the odd flutters in her chest so she could concentrate on his slow instructions. He spoke to her like she was a child, but at least she understood and quickly picked up the motion of the machine.

"You have to watch yourself," the man said.

Helen wrinkled her forehead, not understanding.

"Be careful," he repeated, drawing out the words. "Dangerous. You get your clothes caught, you lose an arm. Maybe get crushed." He mimed an arm being torn off and made a smashing motion with his fists. Helen's eyes widened, and she nodded.

"Good." He motioned to the blonde girl at the machine next to her and practically shouted, "This is Annie. She'll answer any questions."

Annie gave Helen a weary smile, which Helen returned as she got to work.

After only half a day, Helen's arms ached, and she could only imagine how they would hurt the next day when she had to return and do the same thing again. But she had a job of her own! If only she didn't have to owe the job to Demetrios.

She approached the foreman again before she

left.

"Please, I need..."

"You get paid on Friday. Not sooner."

"For Mrs. Alberti. I need a...a paper for my job."

He looked confused for a moment, then nodded. "Oh, for your boarding house lady? I've heard Alberti is a dragon."

He wrote a note in English for her.

Nearly floating, Helen walked home and prepared to face Agatha. As soon as she entered the house, the tension hit her, like a cold wind pushing her back out into the street. Alexander and Agatha sat in the parlor, their faces steely.

"Where have you been?" Alexander asked quietly.

"I went to find work, and I had to start immediately."

"Find work!" Agatha exploded. "What will people say about us? There's enough work around here, and if you're not earning your keep, I'll be charging you for room and board."

Helen took a deep breath. "There will be no need for that. I'll be staying at a boarding house."

Agatha looked ready to explode again, but Alexander cut in. "Is it a respectable one?"

"It's Mrs. Alberti's—where Katherine stays."

"That woman!" Agatha said. "It's unnatural, her living on her own rather than returning to her husband's family."

"Now, Agatha," Alexander said. "When Georgios was killed, the mining company threw her out of his house, and she didn't have anywhere to go. It would be odd for her to live with Demetrios since he's single."

"Demetrios Nikolaides?" Helen asked.

"Her brother-in-law. Or didn't you know?" Agatha asked, her tone accusatory.

Helen opened her mouth to reply but bit it shut again. Of course, she hadn't known. Katherine had talked about Demetrios as if she knew him well, but Helen assumed everyone in Greek Town knew each other.

Alexander gave Agatha a quelling look. "Katherine Nikolaides has to work to earn her keep and to save enough to sail back to Greece. But why do you want to do this, Helen?"

He didn't sound angry, just curious, so Helen took a steadying breath. "I've been thinking about my future. I came here to be a bride. Since then, I've only been working in this house. I'm grateful that you made a place for me, but I can't stay here forever. If I work, I can save up a dowry, help my parents, maybe return to Greece or make a new life here."

Alexander stood, silencing any protest by Agatha, though she looked like she had plenty to say. "We're your family, and we would never want you to see yourself in a disgraceful situation, but I see nothing to object to in your plan. It's a bit unusual, but these are unusual circumstances. When do you go to Mrs. Alberti's?"

"I was going to leave tonight."

He looked pained at that and gave his wife a stern look. "That won't be necessary. You may stay here tonight and move over there at your leisure. We don't want anyone saying our home was not hospitable to our own flesh and blood."

Helen nodded, but she was determined not to stay more than another day. Her new life was calling her.

Chapter Seven

THE NEXT MORNING, Helen left early for Mrs. Alberti's boarding house. She passed through Greek Town and into Little Italy, hardly noticing the transition, except that the smell of bread baking in outdoor ovens faded. Children still played in the streets and the tiny yards in front of their small homes, and women hung laundry in the backyard and gossiped over fences. It was strangely comforting to see the sights she had become used to in Greek Town repeated in her new neighborhood.

She found the address for Mrs. Alberti's home. It wasn't much different from the other houses, though it was a little larger and had an attic with windows.

Helen knocked on the door, and a girl about her age with short black hair pinned back answered.

"Oh, you must be the new girl!" she said in

English. "I'm Maria. Come in. I'll get Mama."

Helen stepped inside. The air was sweet with the scent of basil and tomato, filling her with a warm sense of home.

A matronly woman with streaks of silver in her black braid stepped out of the kitchen. A colorful apron covered her black widow's garb. She wiped the flour from her hands and stepped up to give Helen a keen inspection. Helen stood straight, careful not to flinch under the searching gaze.

"You're Katherine's friend?" Mrs. Alberti asked, her English heavily accented.

"Yes. I am Helen Botzaris."

"And you have a job?"

Helen handed her the note from her supervisor. Mrs. Alberti looked it over and nodded, handing the paper back with a snap of her wrist. "I lock the doors at nine sharp. When you have a late shift, you tell me, and I wait up for you. No men in the house!" She gave Helen a look that made her feel as though she had a young man stashed in her bag. "Except on Sundays, then only in the parlor with at least one other girl. Breakfast is at six. You keep your own room clean."

"Yes, ma'am," Helen said, understanding the drift of the warning.

Mrs. Alberti smiled and patted Helen on the cheek. "You are a good girl."

Helen smiled nervously.

"Maria! Show Helen to her room," she said to the other girl.

Maria smiled at Helen as Mrs. Alberti swept back

into the kitchen. "Don't be afraid of Mama. She's a great cook, and her bark is worse than her bite."

"Thank you," Helen said, deciphering Maria's English idiom with a grin.

"Come on, you have one of the upstairs rooms, right across from Katherine."

Helen trotted up the stairs after Maria, her stomach aflutter. The attic landing was a short hallway with doors on either side. Maria opened the one on the right and gestured Helen inside.

Soft light from the small dormer window fell across a hand-stitched quilt on the bed, a little dressing table with a dusty mirror and a doily, and a worn rug cushioning the bare wood floor.

"It's good," Helen said.

"The bathroom is downstairs—the door next to the kitchen. I'll let you get settled in."

"Thank you," Helen said without looking back.

Maria shut the door quietly behind her. Helen walked forward, running her fingers over the colorful quilt with its careful, hand-placed stitches, then peering out her window into the streets of Little Italy below. A handful of dark-haired boys kicked a ball back and forth in the street, shouting in a mix of Italian and English. Helen watched with a smile, basking in the luxury of her own space, her own special view of the world that belonged to no one else.

The thought of luxury jolted her from her daydream. She couldn't afford this view if she didn't get to work on time. She left her bag on the bed, ready to be unpacked, and hurried down to make the long walk to work. Until she got paid on Friday, she wouldn't be able to ride the streetcar.

She arrived at work out of breath and with a stitch in her side, but she was in her spot when the whistle blew and the giant looms hissed and clicked into life. With time for nothing more than a quick nod of greeting to Annie, her day began.

Helen easily fell into the rhythm of the machines, her hands guiding the loom shaft, and her gaze automatically scanning the cloth for trouble, leaving her mind free to dwell on the little room waiting for her—her own sanctuary. As she watched the machines churn out the huge bolts of woven fabric, she thought what a shame it was that they were all the same. It was fast—so much faster than any human, or even the mythical Athena, could weave— but when they were done, no one would be able to tell Helen's fabric from the fabric of the girls on either side of her, all working in silence. The lack of human voices, the constant hissing and thumping of the machines, and the steady sameness of the brown fabric rolling out in front of her filled Helen with a heavy dullness that she could only shake off by dreaming again of her little window.

By the time she arrived back at Mrs. Alberti's, she was too tired to be interested in more than a few bites of the warm spaghetti waiting for her. She climbed the stairs on aching feet and collapsed into her bed without a thought for the perfect stitching on the quilt.

The week wore on in much the same way, except on Friday, at the end of her shift, when she lined up with the other girls to pick up her paycheck. Some of the American girls talked and giggled with each other, but they took no notice of Helen. Still, she didn't mind them so much when she held her first pay envelope. Money of her very own!

At the bank around the corner, Helen took her place in the long line of factory workers snaking out the door. She grinned at the clerk when she reached the counter. He hardly glanced at her as he took her check and handed her ten dollars.

She carefully tucked the bills into her boot and nearly skipped out of the bank. Ten dollars! Seven dollars a week would go to her room and board, but she could ride the streetcar now—a luxury her tired feet would appreciate—and save some money for herself. In celebration, she rode the streetcar home, feeling sympathy for those who had to walk.

The next few weeks passed in a blur of long workdays, broken only by the peace of Sunday and the excitement of getting paid each Friday. Her bundle of bills grew—money set aside for rent and streetcar fares and a little to send back to her parents in Greece. After a month, she'd gathered enough to spend something on herself. A quick glance in the mirror at her worn-out dress, and she knew exactly what she would buy.

On her next day off, she hoped to take Katherine shopping with her. She knocked on her friend's door.

"Yes?" Katherine's voice sounded weak.

Helen swung the door open to find Katherine curled up on her bed, looking pale. "Are you unwell?"

Katherine hesitated a moment, then nodded, not meeting her eyes. Helen frowned, concerned but not wanting to pry.

"Get some rest, then."

She tucked the blanket around her friend and ventured out on her own.

On her walks around town, she had passed the huge ZCMI department store near the Mormon temple. It looked like it sold everything she could imagine wanting.

She took a streetcar for the short ride up to Temple Square and made her way through the Saturday crowds. She stopped to admire some of the buildings there: the Beehive House, the strange but beautiful temple and tabernacle, and the Hotel Utah, whose Greek columns made Helen smile. She had seen the skyscrapers passing through New York City and Chicago, but she hadn't had a chance to examine them up close. She stood at the bottom of the Deseret Savings building and stared up until her neck ached from watching where the top of the column-like building reached to touch the clouds.

Finally, she turned her attention to the window displays of the ZCMI. The store's sign declared, "America's First Department Store." Its displays were art shows in themselves, with their careful arrangement of clothing, shoes, and machines that Helen didn't know the use of. One of the windows was broken, though, the missing glass boarded over. Someone had painted the letters "KKK" on the board in deep red.

Helen shook off her chill at the strange sight and

hurried inside, then stopped in wonder. She had felt overwhelmed in Demetrios's shop, but now she understood how small it was. Here, she strolled past long racks of identical suits and dresses, along with shoes and even women's underclothing on display where everyone could see them, though none of the other women seemed to think much of it.

Helen made a note of where the dresses were and continued to explore.

A polished wooden staircase in the center of the store led up to the next floor. Through some mechanical miracle, the stairs moved on their own, one side rolling up, while the other cascaded down like a waterfall. Helen paused to stare, letting people push past her. Then she realized she would have to ride those moving stairs to go up to the next level.

She cautiously stepped forward and hopped onto the stairs. The wooden step whisked her upward. She yelped and grasped the moving rail. The girls behind her giggled, but her embarrassment couldn't overpower her awe at the quick trip upwards. The ground floor seemed to shrink away as she watched. She felt like a bird and for the first time believed the stories she had heard that people could ride in flying machines.

The stairs reached the top, and she scurried forward, afraid of being sucked back down by the revolving machine. Other people hurried past her, and she paused to get her bearings.

Shining silver machines surrounded her. Machines for washing clothes, for separating cream from milk, for keeping the milk cold. Sewing machines drew a crowd of women, and Helen watched the demonstrations with them, wincing each time the demonstrator's fingers got too near the rapidly-moving needle. Never had she imagined that there could be so many machines or that they could do so much. A desire to be rich and fill her house with machines seized her mind, but she laughed it off. She had no idea how to use any of them, anyway. And could a piece of metal and gears really get a shirt cleaner than she could, or sew a better stitch? Impossible.

She stared until her head ached from taking it all in, then she rode back down the moving stairs—leaping free of them before they quite reached the bottom—and went back to the women's department.

She looked through the racks of identical dresses, studying the price tags and dropping them quickly when she understood what the dresses cost. Fifteen dollars! More than she made in an entire week. Her eight precious dollars would not last long. She would have to build her wardrobe slowly.

Finally, she settled on a style that only cost seven dollars and was a pretty shade of blue-green that reminded her of the Greek Sea. The stitching was adequate, though the skirt could stand to be re-hemmed. She held the dress up to herself. How did one know if it would fit?

She draped the dress over her arm and wandered among the displays, looking for someone who would help her. Busy clerks talked with other customers and chatted with each other, but each time Helen approached, their gazes slid past her and they would suddenly be busy with something else.

After repeating this pattern for a quarter of an hour, Helen stopped and studied herself in one of the long mirrors hanging on the walls. How wrong she looked, with her long hair and worn out old dress, standing among such luxury with a beautiful dress flung over her arm.

She carefully lifted the dress and shook it out to make certain she hadn't dirtied or wrinkled it. One of the clerks watched her out of the corner of her eye, a smug expression on her face.

Helen understood. Having eight dollars in her pocket didn't mean she would be allowed to buy something in this fine store. How had she not realized she was the only woman in the store with dark olive skin and unfashionably long, black hair? A crow among golden-headed eagles.

She hung the dress on its rack with its sisters where it belonged and walked slowly back toward Greek Town. She glanced at the Greek columns on the buildings she passed. The Americans chose which parts of Greece to love and what part to reject.

But she still needed a new dress. Her old ones would soon be fit for nothing but rags. She worked all day making cloth for dresses she couldn't buy. There was only one place she could shop.

Her stomach tied in knots at the thought of facing Demetrios, but at least he would do business with her. Maybe only his clerk would be there and she wouldn't have to speak to him at all. She pushed the door open, and the bell over the door dinged.

She blinked to let her eyes adjust to the relative dimness and saw the store with new awareness: too crowded because everything a Greek family might need had to fit in one little shop where their business was welcome.

"Miss Botzaris, how can I help you today?"

Helen's stomach plunged at the sound of Demetrios's voice, then fluttered strangely at the thought of his touch when he helped her get her job.

She turned with a tight smile. "I need to buy a new dress."

"I'm flattered you would choose my store," he said, leaning on a display and smiling at her with his dancing eyes.

Her pride flickered. "I was going to shop at the ZCMI, but they..." She stopped. That only made her sound pathetic.

His expression turned serious. "They wouldn't help you?"

The understanding in his voice broke through her defenses, and she shook her head, hot with shame.

"Sometimes you get lucky, and one of their clerks will be friendly, but many of them—"

"Don't even see that we're there," Helen said.

He nodded.

"I understand now, why your store is so crowded," she said.

"Crowded?" He gestured around dramatically with a grin. "I like to think of it as full of possibilities."

"The possibility of an accident if someone trips," Helen said.

Demetrios laughed. "How would you do it differently?"

Helen considered the store and compared it to ZCMI. "You might try grouping things in a way that makes sense so customers can find what they're looking for. You have men's socks next to women's hats. If you put the men's socks on that shelf near..." her face burned as she gestured to the men's long johns. "Well, near their other things, they wouldn't be in the way of ladies looking at hats."

"Good suggestions. I ought to hire you as my window display artist." Mischievous laughter lit Demetrios's eyes. "Then you can put the 'men's other things' in their proper order."

Helen almost had to laugh along with him, but her pride stopped her. "I already have a job."

"That you do. So, you're looking for a new dress? I'm afraid I can't afford fancy female clerks like ZCMI, but I do have some dresses."

Demetrios led the way, and Helen was relieved, after sneaking a look at the price tags, to find that they were all around six or seven dollars. The colors, though, were not as vibrant as the blue-green dress. She trailed reluctant fingers over the fabric.

"They're not to your liking?" Demetrios sounded sincerely concerned.

"Oh, they're fine. I had only...I had been thinking of something in a different color. Something like the sea."

"Ah," he said as if he understood, and Helen thought maybe he did. "What about this yellow? It will look flattering on you, and it reminds me of the flowers in Greece. What I can remember of them, anyway."

Helen considered it. "Yes, that will do. But if it doesn't fit..."

"You can exchange it. We don't have any dressing rooms here."

She nodded, and her gaze traveled again around the chaotic displays. "Why don't you have anything Greek made?"

"Oh, I do. I try to only buy from local mills that hire Greeks."

"No, I mean, things that aren't made by machines. I wove and embroidered in Greece, and some of the Greek or even the Italian wives might make things for you to sell."

"Interesting idea," he said. "Don't you like the clothes we can get here?"

"Well, they're fine, but the stitching isn't always as good, and they're all the same. I suppose I don't like machines as much as Americans do."

"But they'll make your life so much easier!" Demetrios grabbed her by the hand, and she instinctively wrapped her fingers around his. "Come see," he said, leading her to the back.

The other patrons in the store watched them with interest, and Helen thought of Agatha's triumphant disapproval when word spread that Demetrios had led her off who-knows-where. She wriggled her hand free.

"Wait! Where are we going?"

Demetrios looked at her in surprise, then his expression turned to amusement. "Oh, don't worry.

My living quarters are upstairs. This is just the office, and we'll keep the door wide open so the whole neighborhood can spy on us. In fact, I encourage them to. Greek Town could stand to catch up with the times."

He swung open the door to a cluttered room with a desk and a collection of appliances like those Helen had seen at the ZCMI. The other customers wandered up behind Helen to watch Demetrios's demonstration.

"An electric icebox," he said, opening the door to display the cold milk inside. "Saves money by not letting food spoil. This"—he pointed to what looked like a little fireplace with bulbs where the fire would go—" is an electric heater. No more messes from coal." He glanced up at the crowd, his eyes dark, and a bitter edge to his words. "And no more Greek men killed in coal mining accidents. One hundred seventy-one men died in the Castle Gate Mine explosion—fifty of them Greek—and that was just one accident."

The men mumbled at that, their whispers hissing with sorrow and anger still raw from recent losses. Helen remembered Demetrios's brother—Katherine's husband—was killed in that explosion. No wonder he loved his machines.

"These appliances can free us," he went on. "How much money do you men spend paying someone else's wife to do your laundry? This clothes washing machine will do it for you. You can be independent."

"Most of us can't afford such luxuries,

Demetrios," one of the men said, and they drifted back to their shopping.

"One day you will!" Demetrios called after them. He glanced at Helen. "And what do you think?"

She stared for a moment at the washing machine. It was true that she'd never seen him at Agatha's house to collect his lice-infested shirts. She'd never considered why. He didn't need a woman to help manage his home. He could replace her with a washing machine. Make her obsolete. Suddenly, she hated the sight of the inventions.

"I think it's a cluttered mess. I'll just take my dress, thank you."

"What's wrong?" Demetrios asked.

"Nothing's wrong. I just don't like machines. I like things the way they're supposed to be—the way they've always been." She looked away from his wounded expression. "Can I buy my dress now, please?"

She hadn't meant to sound so snippish, and she certainly hadn't meant to hurt Demetrios's feelings, but what could she say? Machines were everywhere—she spent each day hovering over one of them like a serving girl bowing to her mistresses' whims—and they sapped the humanity out of her world. Clothes all looked the same, barely touched by human hands. And she was reduced to just a lever to pull, a button to press—someone who could be replaced at a moment's notice with another set of hands and bored eyes in desperate need of work. She would soon lose herself in such a cold, monotonous world.

Demetrios rang up her dress and wished her a good day. She thanked him dully and headed for home.

Chapter Eight

THE NEXT SUNDAY before church, Helen rose early to put on her new dress, mark the places it didn't hang well, and re-stitch it to fit as a well-made dress should. She studied herself in her little mirror. The dress flattered her, and she looked much fresher and more modern, but she couldn't help wonder how many other women out there wore the same dress.

It was past time for breakfast, so she hurried out of her room to see if there was anything left. Katherine sat on the floor in the hallway, clutching her stomach, her face so pale it was almost green.

Helen rushed forward. "Are you ill? Did you eat something bad?"

Katherine sat back with a weak smile. "No, no, I'm fine. I thought I was past this stage."

"This..." Helen's eyes widened. "Are you...?"

"Yes, I'm expecting my husband's baby." Katherine sat back and closed her eyes. "When he died, I still wasn't sure. He never knew he was going to be a father. He would have been so proud." Tears trickled from under her closed eyelids, and Helen held her and stroked back her hair.

"What are you going to do?" she asked around the lump in her throat.

Katherine opened her eyes and looked up at Helen, her gaze bright with determination. "I'm going to take care of myself and my baby." She wiped her cheeks. "Everyone in Greek Town already thinks I should go back to Greece, to Georgios's family. When they know I'm having his child, they'll probably try to tie me up and ship me back." She gave Helen a pleading look. "But I don't know his parents. I don't want to go back to Greece. I don't want to give my baby to strangers and spend the rest of my life serving them." Her voice became more frantic as she spoke, and her hands fidgeted as though looking for some escape.

"Shh." Helen embraced her again. "You don't have to. We're not in Greece anymore. They can't make you go back." She had never felt any real dislike of her own culture until that moment. "It's going to be all right." Another concern occurred to her. "Does Mrs. Alberti know?"

Katherine sniffled and rubbed her nose. "Yes. I told her as soon as I was sure I was afraid she would throw me out, but she just said, 'I am a widow too.' She'll let me stay as long as I earn my keep. I get five dollars a week from the widows and orphans fund—

from the accident—but that will stop after six years. In the meantime, I'll do housework for Mrs. Alberti and help cook, and... I'll find a way." Her determined look wavered. "I'm scared, though." Her voice caught. "I'm so scared of being alone."

"You're not alone." Helen took her hands. "You have friends: me, and the other girls, and Mrs. Alberti."

"I know. I'm glad." Katherine smiled weakly.

"What about your...your husband's brother? Does Demetrios know?"

Katherine shook her head quickly. "He would tell his parents, and then they would think *they* should have the baby. And me. What if he took me back to them? It's their grandchild, but it's my baby." She hugged her belly. "All I have left of Georgios."

Helen wasn't so sure American-minded Demetrios would send Katherine off to live with strangers in Greece, but she didn't know him as well as Katherine did. After all, he thought a woman could be replaced by a washing machine.

"We won't tell him," Helen said. "You'll be safe."

"Thank you. I had hoped to keep going to the Orthodox church as long as possible, but maybe it's time to stop. I'll go to the Catholic services with the Italian girls instead. I don't think I can hide my belly anymore."

Helen studied her friend. Before, she would have said Katherine had a pleasantly full figure, but now her too-loose dress stretched over her belly. Helen felt foolish for not noticing it before only because she wasn't considering it.

"Yes, do what you have to, to take care of your child."

Helen made the walk to the Greek church alone and sat by herself, keeping her eyes down. Demetrios glanced at her a couple of times during the service. Did he wonder where his sister-in-law was? Did he suspect? Helen wasn't ready to talk to him yet anyway, so she hurried home as soon as the service ended.

That night, Katherine made it downstairs for dinner, though she still looked pale. The Italian girls gossiped and laughed. Katherine didn't join in, but she smiled from time to time. Helen ate her lasagna, relaxing into the daily ritual of dining with her boarding house family.

She caught a sound running beneath the conversation: a shrill whistle. The talk and laughter faded as the others heard it too.

"What in the world?" Maria asked.

They all rushed to the window and peeked out.

A solemn parade marched down the street, their torches bathing the front yards in sharp, wicked shadows. The marchers wore white robes with peaked white hoods covering their faces. They marched perfectly in step, silent except the occasional blast of a whistle. Goose bumps crawled over Helen's skin. The masked men's stern discipline reminded her of the soldiers who had marched through Greece on their way to fight in the Great War. Were they ghosts?

Helen hurried outside, ignoring a cry of warning from Katherine. She wanted to look more closely, to understand the fear that stirred in her at the sight of those men: something primal and animal that made her want to run or to fight. The Botzaris were fighters.

The other girls crowded behind her, peering over her shoulders to watch.

The hooded man at the front of the parade held an American flag high. Others raised crosses or signs aloft. Helen's eyes fixed on the slogans, and she flinched as though the silent words were shouted in her face.

For Race and Nation

Catholics=Traitors

America for Americans

Maria cursed under her breath, and Katherine squeezed Helen's arm.

"Back inside," Mrs. Alberti said, breaking their horrified trance. In her widow's garb, she was almost invisible in the darkness except for her pale, pinched face.

They all hurried in, Mrs. Alberti last of all, and Maria bolted the door. They moved back to the window and watched as the parade marched by, the torches waving fiery streaks in the darkness.

"What was that?" Katherine asked.

"Hate. Fear," Mrs. Alberti said, her voice steely. "The Americans who do not like us are getting bolder. Go to bed, girls. I will keep watch over you tonight."

Chapter Nine

HELEN DREAMED of faceless ghost soldiers burning a path through her village in Greece. She awoke with a headache and forced herself out of bed to peek through the curtains. The street below looked the same, but something had shifted. The life and color had drained from it. There were no children playing.

Helen dressed mechanically and ate breakfast without tasting it. All the girls picked at their food, their faces pinched with worry.

"What do we do?" Maria asked quietly.

"We do not give them power." Mrs. Alberti said. "We don't let them shake us. You get dressed. You go to your jobs."

"Go to work, knowing our foremen might be some of the men behind those masks?" Maria asked.

"Yes. You don't let them stop you. And you don't

strike back in anger. That gives them more power."

Helen was certain the men in the masks already had all the power. Even if the Greeks and Italians wanted to fight back, how could they? She walked to the streetcar station with her head down. The other workers waiting for the streetcar were subdued as well, only speaking in angry mutters until the streetcar arrived.

As they passed beyond Little Italy and Greek Town, the general mood on the streetcar lightened. Americans went on about their day, unaware or unconcerned about the men in the hoods. Helen regarded them with suspicion, but when she studied their faces, she could only see other people like her. How could any of them do something so sinister?

The mood in the shop was likewise subdued, but the machines clacked on. Nothing slowed production as long as the workers were there to push and pull the machines along. Here, at least, she felt safe in her faceless anonymity. When she stepped outside after her shift, she was conspicuous again. Vulnerable.

Helen stepped off the streetcar near Little Italy, and two men got off behind her. She hardly registered them at first, but they walked in time behind her, silently shadowing her path. She rolled her shoulders to shake off her uneasy feeling. Was she just being paranoid? The streets were crowded. The sun had barely dipped below the horizon, and the sky still held its orange glow.

Just to be sure, she took a winding route toward Little Italy. No matter where she turned, the men followed her. Her heartbeat picked up. What did they want? Would they follow her to Mrs. Alberti's? What then?

She whipped around and dove into a restaurant.

"Gotcha!" One of the men grabbed her long hair and pushed her against the wall in the entranceway. "No one in here wants you dirtying up their clean table. Don't you foreigners ever bathe?"

Helen looked around, desperate for someone to come to her defense. A few women with bobbed hair and pearls gave her curious looks, but none spoke up.

"What's going on?" a man in a waiter's apron asked. "I don't want any troublemakers here. You fellows have to go."

The men leered at Helen and stalked away from the restaurant.

"Thank you," Helen mumbled, trying not to let her voice shake.

"You need to leave too," the man said.

"But..." Helen's shoulders sagged at the man's unsympathetic stare. "May I go through the back?"

He nodded and escorted her out. Everyone in the restaurant stared, and she kept her head down, missing the safety of her headscarf. Once outside, she hurried back to Mrs. Alberti's.

Katherine glanced up when she came into the parlor, then stood, her face full of alarm. She put her arms around Helen's trembling shoulders. "What happened?"

Helen poured out the whole story, her voice cracking several times.

"Oh, Helen, I'm sorry."

"I don't understand what I did wrong," Helen said.

"You didn't do anything, except to be different."

Helen sagged against the sofa, thinking of her wish for her headscarf. That only would have made it worse. The markers of Greek respectability did nothing to protect her in America.

"What should I do?" she asked.

Katherine studied her. "We could cut your hair."

"Cut my hair!" Helen smoothed her long, thick locks.

Katherine pulled her hair gently from her hands. "It's beautiful, but it would be lovely in a bob too. And then you'll look more American. Bullies like those men won't pick you out from the crowd so easily."

Helen stroked her hair, remembering how the men had grabbed it, then nodded. "I suppose you're right."

Katherine borrowed a pair of scissors from Mrs. Alberti and carefully trimmed Helen's hair into a neat bob. Helen squeezed her eyes tighter with each snip.

"Now look," Katherine said.

Helen opened her eyes, and her hand went to her head. How strange it felt! Lighter. Chillier. The thick, dark waves of hair framed her face. She automatically brushed her fingers through the bob, but it jolted her to feel her hair stop so soon.

When she put on her hat, she looked extraordinarily American.

"There," Katherine said with a smile. "It's very

attractive on you. You look like a modern, independent woman."

Helen smiled, but her heart was heavy. If she was so independent, why was she letting bullies force her to cut her hair?

She tried to soothe herself by watching the night outside her window. On the eastern mountains, a flickering light caught her eye. A fiery cross stood there like an ominous sentinel overlooking the valley. Helen quickly shut the curtains and sought refuge under her blankets, as though, unseen, the dangers would disappear.

Chapter Ten

THE MOOD AT THE Greek Orthodox church that week was somber. Several men stood guard by the front doors. Fear, anger, disbelief, and sorrow warred in the voices and expressions inside as men and women discussed the recent attacks on Greeks and Italians.

After the service, people gathered in small groups to whisper, like mourners at a funeral. Demetrios cornered Helen. She made no attempt to escape him, hoping, instead, that he could offer some insight that would comfort her.

"Your haircut. It's very stylish," Demetrios said, raising an eyebrow.

"Thank you. It felt...safer."

"Safer? Oh." He stepped closer, and Helen hovered between wanting to lean in and wanting to flee from his nearness. "It will be fine, Miss Botzaris. Those in power in Utah don't want to see these Klansmen succeed either."

"Those in power? The Americans?"

"Do you see all Americans as the same?"

"Well... No, of course not," Helen lied.

Demetrios smiled. "It may look like all those blond-haired Americans are on the same side, but there's a long-standing division here between those who are Mormons and those who are not. Luckily for us, the Mormons outweigh the others in numbers and political power."

"Why is that lucky for us?"

"Because, like us, the Mormons are outsiders."

"But...there are more of them."

"Here, yes. But elsewhere in the country, they are considered odd. The KKK doesn't like them— doesn't like their religion, doesn't like the power they have here in Utah. The Klan has been speaking against Mormons as well."

Helen thought back to the shattered department store window. "Like at the ZCMI."

Demetrios nodded. "You see, everything will be back to normal soon."

"But in the meantime, what happens to us?" Helen asked. "And is normal so good for us, either? Don't you see it? The way people look at us? The way they ignore us or call us stupid and dirty?"

"I see it. I think it will change. In another generation—"

"Another generation! I hope I won't be here."

He touched her arm, his eyes serious. "You have

to give America more of a chance. All you're seeing is Greek Town—a pale imitation of what you left behind. You have to step outside of it to understand what else is here for us."

Helen was aware—too aware—of the firm feel of his fingers pressed against her skin. She didn't understand why it made her thoughts flutter away. "Like what?"

"How about I show you? On a date?" He used an American word.

"A date?" Helen was familiar with the sweet, dark-skinned fruit. "We eat those in Greece too."

He laughed, a rich sound, like the chocolate Katherine sometimes brought home from her job. "It's a different kind of date. An opportunity for a man to take a woman out, so they can get to know each other better."

Helen's face warmed. "Like with a matchmaker?"

"No, just the man and woman, and nothing quite that...binding."

"Of course," Helen said quickly. Stubborn, independent Demetrios wasn't showing interest in her. He was just trying to prove himself right, that his modern American ways, with his hats and machines and dates, were better than her age-old traditions.

"So, you'll let me take you on a date?"

"I don't know."

"You're worried that it's improper? Americans do it all the time, and you're in America now. Ask Katherine."

"Very well. If Katherine approves."

"Good. I'll come for you Friday night at eight-thirty."

"Okay," Helen said, using the very American phrase she heard other girls say.

He laughed again. "Good girl."

Friday night, Helen modeled her new dress in the little dresser mirror. The pale yellow cotton was crisp and clean, but otherwise unremarkable. Helen chided herself for thinking of how she might have looked in the blue-green dress at the ZCMI.

Maria poked her head in the bedroom door.

"You're wearing *that* on your date?" Maria asked, her Italian accent thickened with disappointment.

"It's the best dress I have."

Maria grinned. "Lucky for you, I have this." She produced a dark blue dress that shimmered with sequins.

Helen covered her gasp. "Oh, it *is* beautiful, but I could never wear that!"

"I think we're about the same size, and it's a loose-fitting style."

"I know, but...it has such short sleeves!"

Maria laughed. "I have a shawl that matches it, if that makes you feel better. And it's not as short as a real flapper dress—Mama would kill me if I ever wore a dress like that. Come, I don't have many chances to wear it, so someone should enjoy it."

"Well..." Helen touched the shimmering fabric. It slid through her fingers, silky and tempting as a cup of cool water on a hot afternoon. "I'll try it on."

Maria stepped out long enough for Helen to change. Helen tipped the mirror this way and that, trying to get a better look at herself. It reflected flashes of a modern, almost sophisticated woman, the type who breezed with confidence through the city, flirted with handsome men, and embraced the changes swirling around her.

A stranger.

Maria tapped on the door. "Please, can I see?"

Helen opened the door and stood back for Maria's reaction. Katherine peeked in behind her.

"This Demetrios of yours is going to be floored," Maria said.

Katherine studied Helen with a worried look.

"Is it too much?" Helen asked. "Too...forward?"

Maria laughed. "No, *bella*. It's just more American than you're used to. Here is the shawl. But we need to do something with your hair."

"I have a hat," Helen said.

"No, this dress calls for an uncovered head, or maybe a Greek headdress."

"What?" Helen asked, exchanging a confused look with Katherine. She'd never seen an American wearing a headscarf.

Maria laughed. "I know, these fashion magazines throw foreign labels on things to make them sound exotic—I like to remember how exotic I am while I can beans—but they mean a headband."

Helen patted her hair. How naked it felt! "The headband, then, I suppose."

She refused to wear rouge or paint her lips, but Maria and Katherine fussed with her hair, so by the time Demetrios knocked on the front door, she felt like a paper doll dressed up in clothes cut from a fashion magazine.

Demetrios's eyes widened when he saw her, and then he broke out in a grin that made her blush all the way down to her neckline.

"Be back before midnight," Mrs. Alberti said sternly. She whacked Demetrios with her rolled-up newspaper. "And be a gentleman!"

"Of course, ma'am!"

He offered his arm, and Helen took it, feeling suddenly shy. Her hand fit perfectly against his elbow, and her steps easily matched his relaxed pace, as though they had been strolling together for years.

"I hope you don't mind walking," he said. "It's not far."

"No, I don't mind. It's very pleasant," she murmured. He gave her a self-satisfied smirk, and she hurried on, "I meant to say, it's a pleasant night for a walk."

He chuckled and drew her closer. She almost pulled away, but he was warm in the chilly evening, and the rich, spicy scent of his aftershave intrigued her.

"You look lovely," he said. "Very progressive."

"It feels like a costume."

"I suppose it is, in a way, but aren't we always wearing costumes? Greek or American, orthodox or progressive. We decide every day when we get dressed what we're going to tell the world about ourselves."

"I'd never thought of it that way." But she'd been

aware of it on some level. Wasn't that why she had cut her hair? "Where are we going?"

"It's a surprise. You like music, don't you?"

"Yes, I suppose."

"You'll love this."

He led her out of Greek Town and down a street bustling with people dressed up for the night. Street lights illuminated their path with glowing circles of light, and walking on the arm of a handsome man in a fine suit, Helen felt like a queen.

Demetrios guided her down a side street. The light from the street lamps faded, and she shrunk closer to him in the darkness.

"Don't worry, we're here." His deep voice steadied her nerves and at the same time sent flutters through her stomach.

He stopped and knocked at a door as bland and faded as the others on the side street. A man in a black suit peeked out then beckoned them into a foyer. A rumbling rhythm came from the room behind him. Demetrios exchanged a few quiet words with the man in the suit then guided Helen to the room. When he swung the door open, a wave of drums and brass engulfed her and drew her into the dim space.

The music thrummed through her body, vibrating down her limbs. Despite the foreign rhythms, its bright energy reminded her of dancing in Greece, making her itch to join the crowd on the floor. Men in suits swung around women in short skirts and bobbed hair who moved so smoothly they seemed to be a living part of the music. Bootlegged liquor swirled in glasses and cigarettes hung from the lips of men and women when they weren't dancing. The smoke thickened the air and seemed to swirl in time with the beat.

Helen hovered close to Demetrios, who watched her reaction.

"What is this place?" She shouted to be heard over the music.

"A, uh, jazz club of sorts. A speakeasy, to be honest. Frowned on by some of the stuffier elements of the city, but the music is what matters. It's catching on. Watch."

Helen looked again and began to separate the dancers from the music. Some of the women were definitely flappers, but many wore longer hemlines and longer hair. Not all of them were smoking or drinking. And while many were the white Americans who dominated the city, there were darker heads and darker faces among the dancers—dancing together, swirling into a kaleidoscope under the command of the musicians.

Demetrios drew her aside to a corner of the club where they could hear each other better.

"You see?" he asked.

"You mean, that everyone is dancing together?"

"Yes. The music draws them together, and suddenly it doesn't matter as much, the color of their skin or hair or where they were born. I'm not saying it's going to change quickly, but if those walls can be broken down here, the change will slowly travel everywhere else."

"I suppose it's possible—"

"Not just possible. Guaranteed. No one with white hoods in here. And that's what the Klansmen are afraid of. They know the change is coming, and they are powerless against this."

He gestured to room. The pounding waves of music moved through the crowd, and Helen imagined it moving through the city, flooding the streets, crashing through the factories and the stuffy displays at the ZCMI.

The music turned slow and sultry. Demetrios leaned closer and took Helen's hand.

"Will you dance with me?" His voice blended with the dark, smooth tones of the saxophones. His gaze took hers and held it, and the admiration there thrilled her with a heady rush, like a sip of strong wine. She wanted to spin with him around the floor, free, unafraid.

"I don't know how," she whispered.

"I'll teach you."

He led her out to the floor, and though it was crowded with slowly turning couples, Helen saw only Demetrios and his dark eyes, no longer laughing, but serious and intensely bright. Helen wanted to look away as he wrapped her close, but she stayed staring into his eyes, letting him see her uncertainty, more vulnerable than she'd ever felt in her life. But there was nothing mocking in his intense gaze.

"Just let me guide you," he said, and she did, stepping hesitantly with him, spinning when he turned her, his firm but gentle hands telling her which way to go.

The song ended, and they stood, Demetrios

holding her close. His burning gaze traveled down to her lips, its warmth lingering on her face. She took a breath, shaky with nervousness and anticipation, and closed her eyes. Demetrios touched her face gently, sending warm shivers racing over her skin.

"Come," he whispered. "We need to move for the other dancers."

She opened her eyes, hurt and confused. He looked away, guided her off the floor. Did he not want to kiss her after all? Was he just trying to prove that he was always right, always in control? She followed him with her head down.

"Helen," he said when they sat. "Uh, Miss Botzaris, I should say."

She looked up and forced a smile.

"There's a problem with wearing costumes," he said softly. "Sometimes we let the costume wear us, make us do things we don't normally do. Things we might regret later." He reached out to brush a strand of hair from her forehead, and she leaned into his touch. He pulled his hand away. "I don't want to be a regret. I want to be a choice."

Helen's eyes widened. Were her dress and this place making her do things she would be ashamed of later? She liked Demetrios, didn't she? But he infuriated her at times. She wasn't sure if she wanted to slap him or kiss him, and it certainly wouldn't be right to do both. "I understand," she said.

He exhaled and nodded. "It's hot in here, don't you think? We could go to an ice cream shop if you'd like."

She nodded, and he escorted her out, where the

fresh air brushed away the scents of the speakeasy and made her blush to think of her forward behavior.

Demetrios said little but led her back to the main thoroughfare, where an ice cream parlor attracted couples and teenagers. Helen hesitated to step inside, but in their American costumes, she and Demetrios attracted no unwanted attention. A few of the college boys even gave Helen appreciative stares that earned them a stern look from Demetrios. It felt unreal, to sit eating ice cream like every other American in the room. But did being American mean giving up being Greek? Headscarf or hat, yellow cotton or blue sequins: she could only wear one at a time.

Demetrios returned her home under the watchful eye of Mrs. Alberti with no more affection than a quick squeeze of the hand and left her head swirling with questions.

Chapter Eleven

"How was your time with Demetrios last night?" Katherine asked quietly the next morning. Her belly was growing uncomfortably large, and she rested on the sofa with her feet up on pillows. Her voice sounded vulnerable.

"It was nice. Confusing."

"Confusing?"

"I just...don't know how I feel about Demetrios. Or how he feels about me."

"He always was hard to read. Georgios was so open, so passionate, like he was trying to make every moment count for two lifetimes." Her voice caught, and she was silent for a long moment. "Demetrios was the opposite. He often seemed bitter and so focused on his business, like it was all that mattered. I worry about you."

Helen was quiet for a moment. "You think he's

playing games with me?"

"I don't know. Maybe." Katherine pushed herself up to meet Helen's hurt gaze. "I don't mean that someone couldn't love you, Helen—of course, they could—but Demetrios? Why Demetrios?"

Helen shrugged, stinging at the idea the Demetrios could be using her for some selfish end. Or that Katherine would think so. Why Demetrios? Warmth melted over her as she thought of the way he had held her and touched her, the way his eyes danced when he laughed. Was that something that could be faked?

"I have some errands to run today," Helen said quietly. "Do you need anything?"

"Helen, I didn't mean—"

"I know." She sighed, forcing away her hurt and managed a weak smile. "Do you need anything?"

Katherine sank back into the sofa. "No, thank you."

Helen took her hat and handbag and headed outside. Without thinking, she made her way toward Demetrios's shop. She didn't really need anything. Just clarity. Maybe she could find it there. Maybe she could see the truth in his expression in the daytime, undisguised by smoky music and low lights.

She entered the shop and had to blink several times to make sense of what she saw. Demetrios had reorganized everything. The men's goods sat apart from the women's goods, each neatly organized, and the rest of the dry goods were arranged in their places. It was still cramped, but a sense of order lay over everything. She smiled.

"You like it." Demetrios's low voice rumbled next to her ear.

She gave a start and smoothed her hair back to disguise her embarrassment. "It will make shopping much easier."

"It was an excellent idea," Demetrios said. "A stroke of genius on my part."

Helen's eyes narrowed, and Demetrios winked at her, the laughter back in his eyes.

She chuckled. "Indeed, it was genius."

He grinned. "I have something for you. It just came in."

Helen tilted her head and followed him to the bolts of fabric near the women's goods. He pulled out a smooth length of polished cotton in a blue-green so like the ocean she could almost hear the whisper of the waves.

"Oh!" She ran her fingers over the soft fabric. "How much?"

"I will give you enough to make a dress." When she looked up quickly, a protest on her lips, he added, "As payment for your decorating advice."

She struggled against her pride, then relented. "Thank you," she whispered. "It's beautiful. I often dream of Greece. Of the ocean. It will remind me of that."

"Is that all you dream of?" he asked quietly.

She looked up into his curious gaze. "I suppose," she lied.

"Everyone comes to America with dreams, you know. The question is, what happens to those dreams once they arrive and collide with reality?"

Helen had just wanted a place where she mattered to someone. Was that a dream? It seemed small, and yet at the same time so large that it had left a gaping hole that she wasn't sure she would ever fill.

"Don't try to deny it," Demetrios said, his low voice next to her ear, sending shivers through her and tightening her throat. "I saw it in your eyes as you sat on the train. I think that's why I couldn't stop myself from speaking to you. I wanted to remember how that felt again, just for a moment."

Helen pulled away, flustered by his honesty. "What did you dream of?"

"I thought I was going to come to America and get rich. Return home as a hero. My parents mortgaged their farm to pay the passage for Georgios and me. Imagine, sending a fifteen-year-old and a thirteen-year-old to a foreign land and hoping they would be your salvation!"

"You've done well here."

"Only by shedding all my dreams and taking reality by the horns. When I arrived, I had to pay a Greek labor agent for work. He arranged a mining job for me where I got paid less than the American men working beside me. When your face is coated in coal dust, it's hard to tell what nation you're from, but you could tell by looking at a man's paycheck. The labor agent took a portion of our checks and forced us to spend our earnings at his friends' shops, where they charged us far too much. He lived in the Hotel Utah and wore diamonds while his countrymen died in the mines. Being Greek was suffocating me." He smiled grimly. "I've never forgotten my duty. I send money home to my parents each month, but they will die and be buried, and I will never set eyes on them again."

"You couldn't go back to Greece?"

"Not now. I nearly starved myself to save enough to open my own store where I could charge fair prices and compete with the company stores, maybe drive them under. Being Greek is a burden in America, but at least I could lighten the load for myself and the other workers."

"That's a noble impulse."

"Don't paint me into too pretty a picture. My motivations were mostly selfish. I still thought I could catch some of the promised riches of America—and that those riches would give me security. But owning a store requires a lot of time and investment. Everything I make is reinvested or goes toward covering losses. Comfortable, but never wealthy. And I watch other Greeks come here, and I see the dreams fade in most of their eyes too."

"Most?"

"Yes. There are some that never seem to lose that hope." He studied her face, and she tried not to blush under his scrutiny. "I wish I could understand it. I wish I could capture it again. It felt good to believe. It is life, to have a dream to believe in. Otherwise, we stop living and just...survive."

"You don't think you'll ever find something else to dream of?" It seemed too sad to Helen, to think of someone without any hope. And if he did not hope or dream, then he must have no room in his life for love. What was love but sharing hopes and dreams, pains and failures?

He shrugged. "I… I don't know."

"I have trouble believing that. You still laugh."

"Laugh or cry, I am just lining my gilded cage, pretty bird. But you... You don't have that same silly dreaminess in your eyes that I saw on the train, but there's still something burning there. I keep watching..." he smiled. "I guess I have found something to hope for. I hope that light never dies out."

He touched her hand, and she caught her breath at the rush of warmth that flooded through her.

"Mr. Nikolaides, sir!" The clerk gestured to a man standing in the doorway, shifting from foot to foot. The stranger's fair, freckled skin looked out of place in the Greek store.

Demetrios smiled ruefully and left Helen holding the blue-green fabric, her head in turmoil.

"Do you have any of that Pinkham's Lady's Tonic?" the nervous man asked. "I heard you might sell me some."

Demetrios's eyes narrowed, and he wrapped an arm around the man's shoulders. A friendly gesture, but tension tightened Demetrios's jaw. "Listen to me," he said, his voice low and menacing. "I don't need any of that kind of trouble here. I don't sell the stuff, and I want everyone to know it." He released the man with a bit of a shove.

Helen gave Demetrios a confused look as the other man hunched his shoulders and hurried out of the shop.

"Lady's Tonic?" she asked.

"Mrs. Pinkham's Vegetable Compound. It's mostly alcohol. Medicinal, you see, so it slips under the noses of the Prohibitionists, and moonshiners can use the bottles to hide more potent liquors. But the police are watching us Greeks. The KKK is too. They've attacked people they suspect of bootlegging. I can't afford any rumors about my shop."

Helen nodded automatically, her focus on the worry and frustration in Demetrios's eyes. She suspected it was about more than just protecting his investment. The pain of loss may have made him shield his heart, but she couldn't believe that he had really given up on hope for more from life.

Was that her concern, though? What did she hope for? As she sampled the opportunities America offered, she became increasingly uncertain of what she wanted from it.

Chapter Twelve

HELEN CONTINUED HER ROUTINE, working day after day in the factory. The machines roared on, not caring about troubled hearts or frightening dreams of men in masks. She staggered into work one morning after another night where she couldn't fall into a peaceful sleep. Annie yawned as she took her place beside Helen. Helen yawned in sympathy, aching to go back to sleep.

"Sorry," Annie said, covered another yawn. "I have a colicky baby. If I didn't need this job ..." She shrugged and smiled ruefully.

Helen nodded. The whistle blew, and the noise of the machines grumbling to life drowned out any possible conversation. The shuttle flew back and forth, and the shaft wound the fabric around and around, the never-ending threads always slithering forward. It was hypnotic, and Helen shook herself from a trance, trying to stay focused on her work.

A shrill shriek sounded over the roar of the machines. The whistle again?

Helen looked up to see Annie's face drawn in a terrified scream. Her skirt had caught on the shaft, steadily drawing her in. Annie struggled away from the machine, but a fragile human body was no match for the strength of steel and gears.

Grabbing Annie would do no good—the machine would tear the other girl from Helen's fingers. Instead, she snatched a pair of scissors and sliced the waist of Annie's skirt. The sound of it tearing was lost in the cranking of the factory, but Annie stumbled free. The machine slurped the skirt in, twisting it to shreds until it became so tangled it shuddered to a stop.

Helen dropped the scissors and stared in horror.

"What's going on here!" the foreman shouted into Helen's face.

Annie collapsed, shaking, and wrapped her arms around her exposed legs. Her face was as white as linen as she stared up at Helen with wide eyes.

"Her skirt!" Helen shouted. "It got caught. I cut it free."

She'd done it. The moment had been so fast and frightening, but she had kept her head and improvised. A machine could not have done the same.

The foreman's expression softened. He helped Annie back to her feet and led both women to his office.

"Are you harmed?" he asked Annie.

She stared at him, not seeming to understand.

"I said, are you harmed?" He gave her a little shake.

She gasped and shook her head.

"Okay. We'll find you something to make you decent again and get you back to work." He turned to Helen. "You saw it happen?"

"No, I only heard her scream." Helen shivered. She had only barely noticed the sound over the machines. Annie could have been mauled to death right next to her, with Helen completely unaware.

"And you cut her loose?"

"Yes."

"That's good, quick thinking."

"Thank you, sir."

"I'm not just passing out compliments. I want to make you a supervisor on this line."

"A supervisor, sir?"

"Yes. Overseeing the other girls—especially the new ones. Making sure their work is fast and good, and no more accidents. You'll get a small raise. Are you interested?"

Helen closed her mouth and nodded.

"Good. You'll start tomorrow."

Helen floated through the rest of the day, struggling to stay focused on her work. Annie came back to her machine, though her face was pinched and she didn't look at Helen. In shock. And she had to come back tomorrow with the knowledge of how close that machine had come to crushing her fragile life. Unless she found a job elsewhere, but so many of them were dangerous, especially for those whose English was too poor or whose skin was too dark to work elsewhere.

Well, Helen would help make sure the other girls were safe. Her chest swelled with a sense of purpose.

When she got home, she checked the money she had hidden under her mattress. Now, she would be able to add a little more each week. Already, she had enough to pay for her own little room, living under the same roof with friends. She had enough to send some to her parents, and soon she would be able to help them even more. Or return to Greece herself.

She stuffed the money back into its hiding place. What waited for her in Greece? She had to work hard here, it was true, but she had found a useful role. She worked long days, but her off hours were her own. She could save up enough...for what? A place of her own someday? Classes, so she could polish her English and get a better job? A dowry?

If she were to marry, her money would belong to her husband to do as he pleased with it. Being single was lonely at times, when she lay in bed at night, chilled by the draft from the window and wondering what it would be like to have someone to wrap his arms around her and keep her warm. If she belonged to someone, would he treat her like a possession or a precious gift? Being on her own might be the safest way to live. Yet as she curled up in the cold bed, she wondered if safety was worth the cost.

Chapter Thirteen

THE FACTORY LOOKED DIFFERENT from the perspective of a supervisor. Helen wasn't in charge of much—the men oversaw most of the work—but her line of machines expanded her view of the world a little. Each girl moved like a part of the looms. The machines needed the girls to function properly, but at the same time, the girls were the weak link in the process. Every day, Helen watched to make sure they were staying awake, paying attention. Annie had quit her job a few days after her accident—hopefully moving on to something safer—but the thoughts of what could have happened to her haunted Helen, keeping her always on alert.

One night, Helen rode the streetcar home as usual, almost too tired to keep her head up. It was already dark, but as they passed Greek Town, she saw a crowd rushing and yelling something about fire.

"Stop!" Helen shouted to the conductor, but he ignored her.

When the streetcar slowed to turn, Helen jumped off. She fell and rolled but pushed herself back up and ran for Greek Town, thinking of all of her countrymen who might be in danger.

She stopped and stared when she reached the street where the crowd was gathered. A cross stood in the yard of one of the little Greek houses, with flames slithering up its base and along its arms. The angry red glare of the fire cast long, flickering shadows behind the stunned witnesses. The heat scalded Helen's face as the holy symbol crackled and blackened, smoke clouding the clear night sky.

Neighbors rushed forward with buckets and blankets. Someone kicked the base of the flaming cross, and it snapped like the breaking of bone, crashing onto the patchy lawn. Steam hissed as buckets of water sloshed on the fire, and men and women beat the flames with wet blankets and stomped on embers singeing the grass.

Helen stared in mute horror at the charred skeleton of the cross. A sob caught in her throat, and she swayed into the woman standing next to her: Agatha, with all hostility gone from her face. They shared a wide-eyed glance, and then Agatha caught Helen in her arms, and they cried into each other's shoulders.

Agatha pulled back, reaching for Alexander, who

returned from stamping out the fire. Helen's whole body shook, and she tried to back away. A man with a soot-stained face stepped closer, and she gasped.

"Helen, it's me!" Demetrios said. "It's only me."

Helen stared at him, her hands shaking.

"Are you alright?" he asked.

She shook her head.

"Are you hurt?"

"No, but...why did they do this?"

His eyes darkened. "Because a Greek man dared to marry an American woman. They want our labor and our money, but not us, no matter how American we try to be. Well, they have us anyway." His expression softened. "Let's get you home."

Helen glanced over her shoulder. "It's not close."

"It's not that far. I'll walk with you. I want to make sure you're safe, and it will help me cool off."

She nodded. He paused and touched her chin. She started at his warm caress.

"I thought you said you weren't hurt," he said.

"I..." She touched her chin and found it sticky with blood. "I leapt off the streetcar when I saw the fire. I was afraid for everyone in Greek Town."

He shook his head and smiled, his teeth white against his sooty face. "You never cease to amaze."

She looked down, not sure how to react. Blisters marked his fingers.

She gently lifted his hand. "You burned yourself."

He stared at her hand touching his for a moment then closed his eyes and sighed. "It's nothing. Come along."

He gently tucked her arm under his and walked

her back through the streets. His posture was tense, his gaze darting to every shadow.

"Do you think this is ever going to end?" she asked.

"When we let go of all of our ridiculous old customs and act like the Americans we are, they'll forget we were ever different," he said bitterly.

"You think we have to give up being Greek?"

"If we want to be American. It's fine to come here and earn some money to send back home, keep your head down, and return to Greece. But those who want to stay in America have to become American. It's the only way we'll ever have safety or prosperity—by blending in."

She shook her head. "If you really believe that, then why haven't you become Protestant yet? Or Mormon?"

"Because they don't have the lineage. The authority. The Mormons at least make a claim to it, but the Orthodox Church traces its roots back—"

She chuckled.

"You're laughing at me?"

"I am. You're being ridiculous."

"Me? Ridiculous? How so?"

"You say we have to be more American, but you refuse to give up the most Greek thing about yourself." She lowered her voice. "Besides, I don't think we *can* stop being Greek. Other Americans aren't going to forget who we are, and neither should we."

A frown creased his forehead. "You may be right," he admitted quietly. "But I always hoped if I worked hard enough, I could leave behind 'dirty' and 'poor' and 'foreigner' and simply be judged on my own merits. Certainly, you agree that being Greek holds us back?"

Helen considered that. "There are some things I've learned to dislike about our culture. American women have more freedom—more opportunities. But I'm proud to be a Botzaris. Proud to be Greek."

He looked down. "I'm not sure what being Greek has ever gotten me, except being taken advantage of by mine owners and labor agents. But, working hard and being successful haven't bought me any peace either. I think it just makes these Klansmen hate me more."

They walked in silence for a block.

"Not everything about being Greek is bad," Helen said. "We are fighters, you know. And we have deep roots. We survive."

"Hmm," Demetrios said. They walked on, and he cleared his throat. "Would you consider being courted by an American? Or an Italian?"

"No, I don't think I would. I wouldn't want my children to lose their language or their religion."

"Then I suppose there's at least one good thing about being Greek."

She stared at him, but he looked straight ahead, a smile on his lips. She blushed and looked back down. Was he courting her, then? Her heart warmed at the idea. Perhaps it wouldn't be such a bad thing. He was a lunatic, but he could be a thoughtful one.

Mrs. Alberti opened the door for them, and Demetrios greeted the widow with a nod, which she returned. Demetrios squeezed Helen's hand gently, and his light touch sent pleasant goose bumps up her arm. She smiled a silly farewell at him, and he grinned, handsome even with his face stained in soot.

Mrs. Alberti pulled Helen into the house and looked her over. "You smell like smoke. You've been hurt. What happened out there?"

Helen's giddiness evaporated. "They burned a cross. I fell going to see what happened."

Mrs. Alberti kissed her cheek. "But you got back up, and that's what matters. Wash up. We have another day waiting for us tomorrow."

Chapter Fourteen

HELEN SAT IN FRONT of her mirror, trying out different hairstyles.

Katherine poked her head in the door, her eyes troubled. "You're going out with Demetrios again tonight?"

Helen took a deep breath and nodded. "I know he can be difficult sometimes, but—"

"Wait," Katherine said. "About that. I'm sorry."

Helen turned to face her friend. Katherine sat across from her on the bed.

"I think I've been jealous of Demetrios," Katherine said. "Georgios was. His little brother was more successful than him—opening his store while Georgios stayed at the mine. Demetrios offered him a place at the shop, but Georgios was afraid it couldn't support us, so he stayed at the mine."

Katherine blinked, and tears rushed down her cheeks. "I think he was just being stubborn. Now he's gone. It wasn't Demetrios's fault, but I resented him."

Helen squeezed Katherine's hand. Katherine gave her a teary smile. "And now he's stealing you, and you've been like family to me."

"Oh, Katherine." Helen embraced her friend. "You're better than family to me. You don't make me wash your floors."

Katherine choked out a half-sob and then laughed. "Never. I do want you to be happy, and if Demetrios can offer that to you..."

"I don't know," Helen admitted as Katherine guided her back to the chair in front of the mirror. "I do like him. He's charming and attractive, and he treats me like... like a whole person. But he can be so stubborn, and he seems to want to turn his back on everything Greek."

Katherine nodded. "At least you have the opportunity to make a decision about him." She studied Helen's hair. "Too much curl. Where is Demetrios taking you tonight?"

Helen tried to flatten out her locks. "To a moving picture at the five-cent theater. It's called *The Thief of Baghdad*."

Katherine groaned and curled up around her belly.

"What is it?" Helen asked.

Katherine gasped. "The baby. I think it's coming."

Helen stood, knocking over her chair. "Let's get

you to your room."

Helen helped Katherine across the hall.

"Mrs. Alberti!" Helen called.

Helen guided Katherine to her bed and held her hand through another contraction. Mrs. Alberti and Maria ran into the room.

"It's the baby," Helen said.

Mrs. Alberti nodded. "Maria, go fetch the Greek midwife."

They sat with Katherine, trying to help her find a comfortable position until the midwife arrived. Helen nearly cried in relief at the sight of the old woman with a headscarf over her gray-streaked hair and years of experience etched in her wrinkled face.

But when the midwife felt Katherine's belly, a frown creased her forehead.

"What is it?" Katherine panted.

"The baby. I think it's turned the wrong way."

"What do we do?" Katherine glanced at all of them with frightened eyes.

"We pray. We do our best," the midwife said, but her voice was sad.

Katherine cried out at her next contraction, and the sound rang through Helen, filling her with terror.

A knock sounded on the front door, and one of the other girls called for Helen. Helen reluctantly tore herself from Katherine's side to dash downstairs.

Demetrios stood in the doorway with his hat in hand.

"Oh, Demetrios, I forgot!" Helen said.

Katherine cried out upstairs.

"What's going on?"

Helen hesitated. He didn't know about Katherine, and that was the way Katherine wanted it. But it was his brother's baby in danger. Did he have some right to know the child existed? Especially now, when the baby might not survive? Or would that just cause more pain for everyone?

Katherine cried out again.

"Is that Katherine? What happened?" he asked, taking a step forward.

"It's..." Helen took a deep breath. "Her baby is coming."

"Her... Do you mean she's carrying Georgios's child?"

Helen nodded, feeling like a double traitor at the mingled look of hurt and hope on Demetrios's face.

"She didn't want to be sent back to Greece," Helen said quietly.

"She thought I would want her to go? I want to see my brother's baby."

He took another step forward, and Helen reached out to stop him. "The labor isn't going well. The baby is turned the wrong way. They may not—" Her voice caught. "They may not make it."

Demetrios's face hardened. "I won't allow that to happen."

He dashed back outside. Helen stared after him for a moment then shut the door. Did he know a better midwife?

Another pained cry from Katherine sent Helen racing up to her friend's side. She didn't tell Katherine about Demetrios. They could worry about that later.

The midwife felt Katherine's belly when it tensed with another contraction, and she shook her head. "I do not think we can help the baby, but we can still save the mother."

A sob tightened Helen's chest as she realized what the midwife was suggesting.

"Maria, out!" Mrs. Alberti ordered.

Maria fled, her cheeks pale, and Mrs. Alberti followed her daughter.

Tears rolled down Katherine's cheeks, and sweat glossed her forehead. She tightened her grip on Helen. "Please, I don't want to lose my baby."

"Shh. You're not going to lose it," Helen said. Lied.

The midwife mixed up a drink for Katherine. "Take this. It will help you relax."

Katherine swatted it away. "Save my baby! It's all I have left!"

Another contraction wracked her body, and her belly tightened. They were coming closer together. The midwife shook her head sadly.

"No men!" Mrs. Alberti shouted from downstairs. "No men!"

"Out of the way," Demetrios's voice echoed up the stairwell.

Helen straightened. Did he have a plan to help Katherine? Helen met him in the bedroom doorway. A blond man with a black bag stood behind him, his face grim.

"What are you doing?" Helen asked, glancing between the men and Mrs. Alberti advancing on them like an unhooded executioner.

"I've brought a doctor."

Helen's shoulders sank. "We already have a midwife."

"She needs a doctor, not a midwife."

"No respectable woman wants a man to see her during childbirth," Helen whispered. "Especially an American man! She won't be able to relax or focus. The embarrassment—"

"Foolish woman! Hang the embarrassment and all your silly traditions!"

Helen stepped back, stinging as though he had slapped her. So, that was what he thought of her? Of being Greek? She shook her head and moved to slam the bedroom door on them.

"Wait!" The doctor stepped forward. "I've delivered breech babies before. Sometimes I can turn the infant. There is some risk to the mother, but I might be able to save them both."

The midwife scowled at him, but Katherine lifted her head. "Helen? I don't want to lose the baby."

"This man is a doctor. He can save your baby," Demetrios called over Helen's shoulder.

Katherine stared at him, her eyes glazed.

"He said it would risk Katherine's life," Helen said. "It's not worth it!"

"He'll save your baby, Katherine," Demetrios called as Helen pushed him away.

"Yes, please!" Katherine cried. "Save my baby!"

The doctor squeezed past them, taking off his jacket as he went. He ejected the midwife and slammed the door on all of them. Helen's throat tightened. Shut out.

She whirled on Demetrios.

"You can't promise her that her baby will live!"

"At least I gave them a chance! It's what she wanted."

"You may have killed her!"

He was just like the other men—always thinking he knew what was right, seeing women as something disposable. Helen narrowed her eyes. "You're not welcome here. I'm done with you."

Demetrios's hurt look quickly turned to anger. "Perfect."

He stormed down the stairs, past the wrathful glare of Mrs. Alberti.

Helen tried the door to Katherine's room, but it was locked. She wanted to slam her fists against it, break it down, but what would that accomplish? The worn wood of the door pushed back against her as she slid to the floor. Tears dripped down her face while she prayed. Her ear was pressed against the door, but all on the other side was silent. Like ancient ruins. Like a tomb.

The shrill cry of a baby broke the stillness, and Helen scrambled to her feet, leaning against the door. The handle clicked, and she nearly fell inside. The doctor swung the door open, cradling a squalling baby in one arm. Helen glanced past him. Katherine lay on the bloodied bed, her eyes closed, her face pale and still in its halo of dark hair.

"No!" The scream tore out of Helen. Pain and rage burned from deep in her stomach. She would kill Demetrios. She stumbled forward blindly.

"She's alive!" the doctor said. "I used chloroform to sedate her for the procedure. She'll wake soon."

Helen sobbed in gratitude and collapsed at her friend's bedside. The doctor handed her the baby. A boy. Perfect little hands and feet, wide eyes taking in the brightness of the world.

Helen rewrapped the baby and clutched it to her chest.

"What do we owe you?" she whispered.

"Demetrios paid me."

Helen mumbled a thank you. Demetrios's gamble had paid off, but the price he was willing to pay was too high. She could not bear his arrogance any longer. Yet at that thought, her heart cried out with a loneliness that she knew no cure for.

Chapter Fifteen

HELEN MADE HER WAY to work, keeping her head down. Little Georgios was growing quickly, but Katherine was exhausted from caring for him, and Helen wore herself out helping where she could. It kept her too tired to think about the news of KKK meetings and Greeks arrested for bootlegging. Almost too tired to think of Demetrios.

He watched her at church. She could feel his eyes following her, but he never moved to speak to her, and she would not speak to him, not even when Katherine did. The Greek community understood Kathrine's situation and welcomed her and her baby. Yet every time Helen held Georgios, she remembered that Demetrios had been willing to trade Katherine's life for his brother's baby. His American doctor had succeeded, but that did not mean that his American ways were always right.

She dozed off twice on the streetcar, jerking awake when it clanged to a stop. She avoided the eyes of the other streetcar passengers, afraid that she might see hate in their gazes. How could she know which of them went out at night with white hoods and terrorized the immigrant neighborhoods? They might harass her there in broad daylight, too, and she couldn't be sure anyone would stand up for her. America did not want her.

She got off the streetcar and walked a block before she became aware of yelling. Afraid of what she would find at the factory, she hurried forward, peering around the corner of a building. A group of men with signs stood in front of the entrance to the factory, shouting and shoving away anyone who approached. Another woman who worked on the looms walked up beside her and stared at the mob.

Helen glanced at her. "Are they the Klan?"

The woman gave her an odd look and shook her head. "I don't think so. It looks like a strike."

"A strike?" Helen looked back at the men and recognized some of their faces from the factory. They looked so different—no longer tired and sweat-drenched, but angry and determined. "What are they striking about?"

The other woman shrugged. "Safer working conditions or higher pay."

Helen nodded. It would be good to make the looms safer, and there would be fewer accidents if they didn't have to work such long hours or had more breaks.

"We get paid less than the men," Helen said.

"And today, we get paid nothing at all."

Helen gave a start. Of course. The men weren't going to allow the women to go into work either. No work meant no pay.

"What do we do?" Helen asked.

"Join the strike or go home. My husband's not going to be happy. We need the money."

The woman walked away. Helen watched the striking men a few more minutes then turned back. She could afford a few days without work, maybe. She had some savings. And Mrs. Alberti wasn't unkind; she would let Helen be late on the rent. But unless Helen was going to move back in with Alexander, she had to have income.

Yet the strike dragged on. After the first week, Helen looked for another job, but with the glut of workers, no one was hiring. The neat little roll of bills she had saved thinned. Soon, she would have to make a choice about what to do.

"I heard of a place hiring laundry workers," Katherine told her one morning as she rocked Georgios. "If you hurry, you might be able to get the job."

"Thank you!" Helen put on her hat and gloves and ran to the address Katherine gave her, instead of waiting for the streetcar. She arrived out of breath, taking just a moment to smooth her frizzled hair before stepping up to the counter.

"I heard you were hiring laundry workers," Helen said.

The man didn't even spare her a glance.

"Position's filled."

"Oh." Helen's hope turned to ash in her mouth. "I see. Thank you."

Helen walked out, hardly seeing where she was going. Tears clouded her eyes, but she quickly wiped them away. She sat on a bench in a park and watched the children playing. What was she doing, crying over not being hired to do laundry?

It wasn't just the job, though. She liked being independent. Being able to choose. Yet for every step she took, something pushed her back two. Everywhere she looked, the promise of America seemed to be for someone else. Someone who spoke English better, without an accent. Someone who went to the right church, who had the right name, like Nelson or Smith. America, it seemed, was not for her, and she was running out of choices.

She could move back to Greek Town with Alexander and wash laundry for strangers, or she could go back to her village and work for family.

The roll of bills under her mattress might still be enough to provide her own dowry after paying for her passage back to Greece. The travel office was just around the corner. At least, she could find out what it would cost to go home.

She approached the counter, trying not to clutch her hands together like she was pleading.

"How can I help you, miss?" the man asked.

"How much are tickets to Greece?" She was proud that her English had improved enough to have this conversation, though she could never shake her accent.

The man checked his book. "The train ticket from Salt Lake City to New York City will cost sixty dollars, plus an extra ten if you want a berth to sleep in. That's changing trains in Denver and Chicago. The steamship passage is thirty dollars."

Helen tried not to gasp, but she felt like she'd been struck. Maybe he was trying to sell her first-class accommodations. "Is that for second-class rail and steerage on the ship?"

"Yes, miss."

"Thank you." Helen wandered away from the counter in a daze. Ninety dollars! Yiannis had paid so much just to bring her to Utah.

She found herself circling downtown, walking around the temple and the tabernacle, then up the hill to the Catholic church. The lush green lawn invited her to sit and look out over the city. How much money had she saved? Maybe forty dollars. Fifty dollars short, and that was if she left immediately and returned home with empty pockets. But what was she to do? If she stayed, her resources would dwindle until she had nothing left at all.

She stood and slowly walked toward the boarding house. It wasn't close, but even the small charge for the streetcar seemed like too much when she realized how dire her financial straits had become. How much could she earn if she took in some washing? Did she have anything she could sell?

She finally made her way back to Mrs. Alberti's.

"What's wrong?" Katherine asked when Helen collapsed onto the sofa.

"It's…I can't find a job. I'm not sure what to do.

I'm not even sure if I should stay here in America."

"Oh," Katherine said softly, bouncing Georgios.

"Do you ever think about going back to Greece—on your own, not to live with Georgios's parents?"

"Sometimes. For now, I get the widow's stipend, but after that ends, I don't know." She met Helen's eyes. "But what's right for me isn't right for you. I'll miss you if you have to leave, but we can write, and maybe you can find a place for me if I come back too."

No more certain, Helen went upstairs and opened the bag she'd brought from Greece. She lifted out the jewelry she would have worn at her wedding. It was dull with dust, but she polished it until it shone again.

How long ago it seemed that she had arrived in Utah, thinking she was here to be a bride. It seemed silly now. What kind of life would she have had with Yiannis? It might have been a happy one, but she would have missed out on the adventure of working for herself, living on her own, befriending Katherine and the other girls at Mrs. Alberti's.

She packed the clothes and linens away. Her headscarf still looked pretty and fresh since she had not worn it for long. It would do nicely if she returned to Greece. She held up the jewelry and drew a deep breath. Now for the difficult part. She had to face Demetrios again.

Helen was certain her jewelry had value, but no one would appreciate it as much as another Greek, and she wasn't sure who else to go to. She might not get enough to pay for passage to Greece, but it would be enough to survive on, maybe enough to move somewhere where there were more jobs until she could save more. This was probably the last time she would have to deal with Demetrios. She didn't understand why her heart ached at the thought.

On the walk to his shop, she savored the transition from Little Italy to Greek Town—the subtle shift in the colors decorating the houses, the clothes hanging out to dry, the scents of roasted lamb and baking bread. A few acquaintances in Greek Town greeted her, but she tried not to linger long enough to talk. If she was leaving, what was the point of making it harder?

She reached the door of Demetrios's shop and stopped to straighten her hair before pushing the door open. The little bell over the door sang its welcome. Demetrios looked up from his counter, surprise registering on his face before he hurried forward to greet Helen.

"I've been hoping to see you," he said. "Katherine is well?"

Helen flinched a little at the reminder. "She is."

"I know you're angry, but I would trust that doctor with my life. The life of my family too. I knew he could save them both."

His words twisted in Helen's chest. Of course, he trusted in the modern, American doctor, and Katherine was grateful that he had. Perhaps he had been right, but he didn't need the opportunity to gloat, especially not after he had called her foolish. She shook her head.

"I didn't come to talk about that."

He looked confused. "Then what can I do for you today?"

"I have a few things I need to sell," she said quietly, holding out the jewelry.

He lifted a necklace to study it in the light. "You mean you wish to pawn them? I can hold onto them for a month or two."

"I don't think I'll be back for them."

He looked up quickly, and she expected a barrage of questions or a lecture. Instead, his eyes looked pained. "What has happened, Helen?"

His gentle voice nearly broke her. "It's... I'm thinking of going back to Greece. I can't do this anymore. The Klansmen. The dirty looks on the street. And the strikes shutting down the factory. If I don't go now, I may be trapped."

He watched her intently. "It will get better, you know. Things turn dark, but the sun rises again." He hurried behind the counter and pulled out an English newspaper. "Look at this. The *Deseret News*. They condemn the Klansmen and their secret societies. And they're speaking for the Mormon church leaders too. A few angry men won't last long against that kind of social clout. Soon, everything will be peaceful again. You have to admit America isn't all bad."

"It's not, but neither is Greece." Helen studied the newspaper, picking out the many words that she knew. "I'm glad things are getting better, but I can't wait for it. How will I live? I can't go back to Alexander's again." She shuddered. "I won't. At least this way I have the freedom to pick my life's direction before I run out of choices." Her gaze pleaded with Demetrios, asking him to understand.

He cleared his throat and looked at the jewelry again. "I can give you sixty dollars for these. And I will hold them in pawn for you, in case you change your mind."

Helen was too stunned to object. She took the bills and almost walked into the street holding them out in her hand, until she had the presence of mind to stuff them into her shoe. Sixty dollars! She could live on that for quite a while longer, or she could leave tomorrow. Demetrios's generosity opened up a world of options for her, and she didn't know what to do with them.

She wanted to be home. But where was her home? She closed her eyes. Blue-green waters. Villages where sheep roamed in the streets and girls fetched water from wells. Where things were simple, and the sun shone in a way it didn't anywhere else. Just before she opened her eyes, she pictured a pair of dark brown eyes laughing, but she shook that image away.

Everywhere she looked in America, doors closed. The choices that had seemed almost ripe enough to pick withered before she could pluck them. She had no choice but to return to Greece before she ended up in poverty, with all of her choices gone.

Chapter Sixteen

HELEN WENT TO CHURCH the next Sunday wearing her headscarf. If she was going to return to Greece, she had to give up her American customs. The scarf didn't sit right on her short hair, though, and she missed the brim of her hat shading her eyes.

She paused on the street in front of the newly-completed Orthodox church, the white granite Corinthian columns gleaming bright and steadfast in the face of prejudice. Yet the cross-shaped building was made of red American brick, as if uncertain if it belonged in Greece or Utah. Or maybe it was comfortable being some of both.

Helen shook herself. She was happy for the Greeks in Salt Lake City, that they had such a church, but it didn't mean that her place was here.

As she waited for the service to start, she

overheard two men arguing.

"Strikes only hurt us. We either go without being paid or work as scabs and everyone hates us."

"Ha! We have fought for freedom from the Ottoman Empire for centuries. Here, we fight to be treated fairly, and things are improving. But we do have to fight. We have to sacrifice."

The first speaker noticed Helen watching and gestured to her. "Miss Botzaris, you're out of work because of the strike. What do you think of that?"

She was too astonished at being a part of their argument to find her voice for her moment, but then she said, "The factory was dangerous. Too dangerous. It hurts to have no pay, but...yes, it is worth it if it makes the work safer for everyone."

"Ha!" the second man said. "You see, the proud Helen Botzaris, she knows how to fight."

Helen took her seat. Proud, was she? She was proud to be a Botzaris. Proud to be Greek. She was proud to have worked to support herself.

Was she too proud to admit when she had been wrong about America? About Demetrios?

Too proud to fight for what she really wanted?

The question worried her all through the service, whispering doubts in her ear as she tried to listen to the priest. When it was over, she scanned the crowd for Demetrios. She didn't really have anything to say to him.

He had called her foolish.

He had saved Katherine's baby.

He had infuriated her with his arrogance.

He had made her see things in a whole new way.

Helen caught a glimpse of him in the back of the church, but he was heading out the door, already gone.

She stood alone in the crowd, the buzz of conversation a hollow ringing in her head. This wasn't her world anymore. Or, was it Greece that she had left behind without fully stepping through the door into America?

She slipped outside and squinted through the dirty air of the city, memorizing the spires of the Mormon temple and the round dome of the capitol building imitating the splendors of ancient Greece. The sunlight in Greece was different—brighter and more golden—and she invited the memory of it to warm her, but the image was too watery and dim. Now, it was the light of Utah's sun that heated her skin.

Her feet guided her through Greek Town, and she tried to imagine saying goodbye as she walked. Outdoor ovens baked Greek food, while electric lights and running water indoors made life a luxury. Could she go back to hauling water and obeying her male relatives, no longer working for herself and her own dreams? What was it that had brought her to America?

The air was rich with the lingering scent of coffee and baking bread. Underneath it, the faint scent of something burning tickled her nose. Not like roasted coffee beans, but the strange, acrid stench of scorched wood and fabric.

A fire! And while everyone else was at church. She broke into a run, following the scent through

Greek Town. To a street she knew.

To the front of Demetrios's store.

Smoke rolled up inside the shop windows. A fiery-red painted cross slashed across the front of the building, and the door hung loose on its hinges, glass scattered on the ground. Had Demetrios stumbled onto Klansmen in the midst of their vandalism?

"Demetrios!" Helen shouted. "Demetrios!"

She stepped inside. Smoke filled her nose and made her eyes water.

The shop was in disarray, the electric heater tipped onto a smoldering rug—the source of the smoke. In a few moments, it would burst into flame, and everything inside would be ash. She tore off her headscarf and ran out to drag it through the filthy water in the gutter. With the scarf over her mouth and nose, she raced back into the smoky building.

"Demetrios!" she screamed, her voice deadened by the scarf.

She tried to peer into the back office, but she couldn't see through the smoke. She pulled her scarf from her face and battered the smoking rug with the wet fabric. It hissed and sizzled, and more smoke billowed up from the floor. She hit the rug again and again, remembering the men who put out the flaming cross with their coats.

"Helen!" a muffled voice called.

She glanced up for a moment and saw Demetrios run into the shop, a handkerchief tied over his face. He thumped his damp jacket over the rug, and Helen swatted at smoking spots with her scarf.

Shoulder-to-shoulder, they battered the smoldering rug as it threatened to burst into flame. Finally, the smoke thinned, and the sodden rug squelched underfoot. They both sat back, gasping for air.

"Outside," Helen said.

Demetrios nodded and took her hand. She squeezed it back and led the way outside. She took a lungful of clean air, but before she could enjoy it, Demetrios threw his arms around her, squeezing her breath out. Too stunned to pull away, she gave in and leaned into the comfort of his chest.

"Helen." He pulled away. "What were you thinking? You could have been killed."

"Me? I thought you were in there! I couldn't lose you!"

He stared at her, and the look in his eyes sent a warm flush over her cheeks.

"Do you mean that?" he asked quietly.

Did she? She had come to American looking for her home—a home worth fighting and sacrificing for—and it had seemed all of her dreams were turning to smoke and ash when she saw the fire.

Warmth started in her heart and spread down every limb. "Yes, Demetrios."

"Helen," he breathed, and he embraced her again. "Maybe you *are* a foolish woman." She pulled back, but he laughed and added, "and I am a foolish man. A foolish, stubborn man. Forgive me?"

She nodded and let herself melt into his arms.

"I was so afraid you were going to leave," he whispered.

"But you were the one who made it possible."

"I know. That's what made it all the worse. But I wanted you to choose. I wanted—I dared to *hope*—you would choose me."

She leaned back to look into his eyes, seeing there the reflection of his humor and his seriousness, and memories of warm conversations, dancing in the speakeasy, leaning on his arm when she was frightened. "I do."

He ran his fingers over her cheek, sending shivers through her core. She tilted her face up to him. He kissed her forehead, the tip of her nose, and then his lips found hers.

Helen pulled him closer to keep her knees from buckling, not caring that they were standing on the sidewalk and anyone could see them. They were in America, and he was a good Greek man.

Demetrios pulled away, his eyes laughing. "You know, I have some beautiful bridal jewelry in pawn, though it probably needs to be polished again now."

"You don't expect me to buy it back!" Helen said, laughing breathlessly.

He grinned down at her. "I'm willing to return it as a gift on our wedding day."

She smiled up at him, thoughts of their future together filling her with the warmth of hope and soothing the pain of her past fears and longings. "You have a deal."

"But I suppose we'll have to buy you a new headscarf," he said, twirling a strand of her loose hair around his finger, and nearly making her mind numb at the distraction.

"Never mind that," she murmured. "I prefer hats."

Epilogue

"THEY'RE COMING!" Demetrios called up the stairs from the shop.

Helen and Katherine glanced at each other and quickly put away their paintbrushes. Decorating Katherine's new room would have to wait. Helen dashed across the hall to her and Demetrios's bedroom and pulled out her old headscarf—scorched in places but clean and beautiful to her, rich as it was with memories of Greece and America. She met Katherine and little Georgios in the hall. They trotted downstairs to wait by Helen's favorite display in the newly-restored shop: the items handstitched by local Greek and Italian women.

Demetrios took Helen's hand, running his thumb over her knuckles to give her pleasant goose bumps. "No hat today, Mrs. Nikolaides?"

"Today, I want them to know that I am Greek."

He nodded, and together with Katherine, they hurried a few blocks to where Greek Town intersected with Little Italy. A crowd of Greeks and Italians had already gathered, silent and somber as they lined the street. Demetrios helped them wriggle their way through to a spot next to Alexander and Agatha. Helen waved to Mrs. Alberti and Maria across the way, but then they all turned their attention to the slow parade of white-hooded men marching up the street.

The men's silent march sent chills racing over Helen to settle in an icy lump in her stomach. Katherine clutched baby Georgios close, and Demetrios tightened his grip on Helen's hand.

A quiet group gathered behind the marching men: Greek and Italian boys in their Sunday finest. The parade passed into the heart of the watching crowd, and a shout went up. The boys darted forward through the parade. As they did, they grabbed robes and hoods, pulling them up and knocking them off. The marchers stood unmasked in the center of the neighborhood.

The crowd of Greeks and Italians pointed and laughed.

"Look, it's old Mr. Magnusson. I guess we won't be shopping at his store again."

"Henry Bean! Anyone here work for Henry Bean? Don't bother going in to work for him tomorrow. We all quit!"

"It's George Townsend! And he likes to sneak down to Greek Town for a coffee. We won't serve him anymore."

The Italian band struck up a lively tune, drowning out the feeble attempts of some of the Klansmen to restore order. A few tomatoes flew as the men struggled to get their robes back on. They ran off, their heads covered, and the crowd broke up into circles of celebration.

"Do you think that's the end of it?" Helen asked.

"Maybe." Demetrios draped his arm around her waist, and she snuggled into his embrace, fitting perfectly against him. "We've taken away their power of fear, at least," he said. "Now they know we won't be chased off."

Helen glanced around the crowd. Katherine held Georgios and smiled as she spoke with Maria and some of the ladies from church. Alexander laughed with a group of Greek men, while Agatha watched her children dodge around the legs of the adults. The scent of basil wafted over them, making the autumn sunlight feel warmer. In the distance, streetcar bells clanged. Helen smiled up at Demetrios.

"No, we won't. This is where we belong."

Author's Note

HELEN AND DEMETRIOS are fictional characters, but this novella is based on actual events in Utah in 1924.

In 1900, the US census listed only three Greeks in Utah. By 1910, there were several thousand Greek men drawn by the opportunities for work in the mines and railroads, but only a handful of Greek women. Many of the men had only come to America to earn money to support their parents or families back home in Greece, but some decided to stay and sent for "picture brides" to come to Utah and marry them after exchanging pictures (not always their own!). The women were willing to make the dangerous journey because Greece was struggling with the effects of economic depression and war, and without dowries, they could not find husbands in Greece.

The Greeks in Utah, as in the rest of America, faced prejudice because of their ethnicity, language, and religion. They were paid less than American-born workers and often worked in the most dangerous jobs. They had to pay bribes to wealthy Greek labor agents like Utah's Leonidas Skliris for these less-desirable jobs.

Though the KKK opposed Utah's dominant Church of Jesus Christ of Latter-day Saints (Latter-day Saints or Mormons), it still found a foothold in Utah for a time, even among some Latter-day Saints. The KKK attacked Greeks and other immigrants, burning crosses on hillsides and in yards (such as the Greek man who married an Anglo American woman), and vandalizing businesses suspected of selling bootlegged liquor. Despite Utah's straight-laced reputation, it had its share of speakeasies and moonshiners during the 1920s.

The Castle Gate Mine disaster remains one of the top ten worst mine disasters in United States history, and the second-worst in Utah after the Scofield Mine disaster of 1900. Over 170 men died in a series of explosions in the Castle Gate Mine in March of 1924, including Greeks, Scots, Englishmen, Italians, Welshmen, Japanese, Austrians, Anglo-Americans, and African-Americans. The mine had recently laid off many of the single men due to a drop in demand for coal, so it was mostly married men with children who were killed. Unlike the Scofield Mine disaster, the widows and orphans of Castle Gate were awarded a small monthly stipend.

Factory work during this time was dangerous for all workers, and unions to protect workers' rights were discouraged in Utah. Despite this, there were occasional strikes—especially among miners—as workers sought better pay and safer working conditions.

Despite these hardships, the Greeks and other immigrants persisted. The first Greek church in Utah, built in Salt Lake City in 1905, became too small to serve the Orthodox community, so the Greeks bought land to begin the Holy Trinity Greek Orthodox Church in Salt Lake City in 1923, which still stands today. This church is the only remaining building from what was once a thriving Greek Town in Salt Lake City.

Though the descendants of these Utah Greek immigrants are now fairly assimilated into mainstream culture, they remain proud of their heritage and hold an annual Greek Festival in Salt Lake City.

To learn more about the Greek experience in Utah, I recommend the writings of Greek American historian and Utah native Helen Papanikolas, especially *An Amulet of Greek Earth* and *A Greek Odyssey in the American West.*

Acknowledgments

THANK YOU to my critique partners in the Cache Valley chapter of the League of Utah Writers, UPSSEFW, and the Clandestines—you constantly push me to be a better writer. Thanks to Heather Maloney for beta reading. I also owe a great deal to the late Helen Papanikolas for her research and writing on the Greeks of Utah. And, as always, I couldn't do any of this without my wonderful family and all of their support.

About the Author

E.B. WHEELER attended BYU, majoring in history with an English minor, and earned graduate degrees in history and landscape architecture from Utah State University. She's the author of eight books, including Whitney Award finalist *Born to Treason*, *No Peace with the Dawn*, *Letters from the Homefront*, and *Utah Women: Pioneers, Poets & Politicians*, as well as several award-winning short stories, magazine articles, and scripts for educational software programs. The League of Utah Writers named her the 2016 Writer of the Year. In addition to writing, she consults about historic preservation and teaches history at USU.

www.ingramcontent.com/pod-product-compliance
Lightning Source LLC
Chambersburg PA
CBHW071924220626
47052CB00002B/441